HUNTER

CAMP GOLDEN HILLS

THE MYSTERY OF MIKEY

DANIEL CURRIER

Bird Man

Thien

BUTTERBLAZE
PUBLISHING

Copyright © 2019 by Butterblaze Publishing

First Edition: June 2019

ISBN 978-1-73310-122-6

Library of Congress Control Number: 2019905361

For my Family

GOODIE, YOU'RE HERE

I was very annoyed about going to some lame summer camp for a whole fourteen days. My mom and dad were getting divorced, and this was their way of keeping me out of it. While they argued over who got the "nice" plates, I was shipped off to Golden Hills summer camp to have some "fun."

Golden Hills was a large camp, full of activities like shelter building, nature walks, boating, archery, arts and crafts—all the things you would expect from an overnight summer camp. The camp even had a little gift shop that sold snacks like soda, chips, and candy.

The drive took an hour and a half just to get to the main gate, and the whole ride I was lost in my thoughts. School being over, whether I had any real friends, my parents constant arguing, and the general terribleness that was my life. Well, maybe that was an exaggeration. I mean, it wasn't that bad compared to some stories I'd heard. But before being shipped off to camp, I'd been looking forward to just being huddled up in my room for the summer with my cat.

How long is this drive gonna take?

"Mom, when are we gonna get there? I'm starving," I complained.

"You're not starving. You just had a whole bucket of fried chicken. You're gonna get fat if you keep eating like that," my mom said.

"I can't get fat, Mom," I responded. "I'm skin and bone!"

The car hit a speed bump as it turned into the entrance. "We're here!" she exclaimed.

I sat in the car, not wanting to get out. She sat in the car too—probably wrapped up in her own thoughts. She got out of the car and opened my door for me, encouraging me to exit. I stepped out and the sun was blinded me.

Wow. Vermont is really sunny.

It was the late afternoon, though, and the sun was just at that angle that made everyone hold their hands up like they wanted a high five.

"Here, put on some sunscreen," my mom said as she smeared my face with cold white sunblock.

"Mom! Come on! I don't need this!" I said a little louder than I'd intended.

"Of course you do. You burn like crazy!" She continued to reach for my face.

Ugh. Why does she still treat me like I'm three and not thirteen?

This was how I walked into summer camp—with sunscreen clumped all over my face. It made me look like an idiot, and I couldn't rub it in or my hands would be covered too. This was going to be the worst first impression ever. Arguing about it was pointless though, and my mom had enough grief of her own.

From the car, I could see the main lodge, where I needed to check in. It was a large building, kind of like a log cabin but more modern. It still looked fairly worn down with age. I noticed something else that did not look quite right: the main entrance sign identifying Camp Golden Hills was all rusted and flimsy.

That can't be a good sign. Oh geez, I'm making puns in my head. I better get them out quick before I talk to anyone.

"Why hello there, camper! Are you ready for two weeks of fun?" the camp director shouted as he walked toward us. I didn't respond to his greeting, and that was a mistake because an ice-breaker joke came right after.

"Hey, did you know that you can't run through a campsite? You can only ran—because it's past tents!" He had to stop and catch his breath from laughing at his own joke. I groaned.

I got my backpack and sunglasses from the back of the car and my mom said goodbye. I loaded my gear into the carts in the parking lot. Parents were discouraged from walking campers to the campsite. I was hoping my mom didn't make a stink about escorting me to my campsite. "Have a good time! I'll see you in two weeks. Make sure to write me a letter or two! I love you so much," she said as she gave me a big hug and kiss.

The hug lasted embarrassingly long, but it felt like she needed it more than I did. As the ranger and I started off toward the trail to the campsite, I looked back at my mom. She was still standing in the parking lot waving at me. She looked relieved that I had turned around one last time. I stopped walking and gave her a wave back. I could see how happy that made and her and she blew me a kiss. Maybe these two weeks would not be as bad as I'd thought. I caught her kiss in mid-air. She'd done that when I was little. It was crazy how so much had changed.

The camp director brought me to a campsite in the woods that was about a ten-minute walk from the parking lot. His name badge said he was Glen, but I guess me not laughing at his joke got him out of a talking mood. We arrived at the site which had a sign reading "Sleepy Hollow" nailed into a tree.

Interesting. I just read a book with that in the title not too long ago.

Read might have been an overstatement. Mostly I skimmed notes on the computer after doing some mad searching online. That's where I stumbled onto Camp Golden Hills camp. According to their website, the camp had just celebrated ninety years in operation. It was a 1,600-acre camp with a 100-acre pond. It had about a dozen different campsites with five tents in each. Each tent held 2-3 campers, and each campsite was meant to be age specific.

Sheesh, why do I even remember that? Why can't I remember random facts like this when I'm taking tests at school?

As I walked up, I noticed other campers had already arrived. There were about two dozen others chatting around the main firepit area. They looked to be about the same age as me, some were maybe a little older. My eyes started wandering, trying to take in the surroundings, and landed on a poster on a tree that read, "Goodie you're here!" I rolled my eyes.

Wow, how corny. This whole thing was going to be corny.

The ranger directed me to my tent. I dropped my bag at the entrance of my tent, eager to check out my living space. The tents were military grade and were big. I was surprised that we didn't have to set up anything. They were built on platforms about two and a half feet off the ground. I pulled back the thick flaps and poked my head in.

Inside they had tiny little cots. There were two of them with only a mattress and nothing else. I grabbed my stuff, climbed into the tent, and started pulling things out. A bug net and clothes bin, which I slid under my cot, a mess kit, lantern, flashlights, batteries, and more of the typical camping stuff. Wow, my mom sure packed a lot of batteries.

I shoved all the extra stuff under my cot, though it was pretty crowded under there. Boy, it was hot in here. I wish they had put the tent flaps up so it would be cooler at lights-out. I mean, that was just basic camping knowledge. The camp director stopped by and said to come out to the firepit once my gear was settled. I took a deep breath to clear my head and ventured out.

Here goes nothing.

Benches crafted from tree trunks were laid out in a big circle around the firepit. I sat down next to a big kid who had clearly never missed a meal.

"Whaz up?" he asked.

I wasn't really paying attention. "What?"

"Whaz goin' on?" he said. I was so confused. This kid looked like a melting potato. He talked like one too.

"Uh, not much," I replied.

"Oh thaz cool man. Me, I juzt be chillinz," he said with a big smile on his face. Clearly, this kid had no idea that the letter "z" was not in every word in the dictionary.

"Um, okay." I kept my head down. I wasn't really a social kid these days, but we were not allowed to stay in the tents. I just stared down at my hand, waiting for something interesting to happen.

Just then one of the camp counselors yelled out, "Hello, campers! Are you ready for some fun?"

Everyone except me screamed at the top of their lungs, "Yeah!"

The counselor whose name tag read Bill then said, "That's great to hear! This week and next week we'll be starting our traditional Red Team versus Blue Team competition—"

"Which Red Team has been dominating for many years now!" another counselor yelled.

I rolled my eyes. I looked around at the crowds of people that were gathered around. I wasn't a fan of big crowds. The sun was setting now, but I was still blazing hot. I tugged on my shirt.

"But first, we're gonna line up to go to the registration lodge to fill out your medical forms and other paperwork!" Counselor Bill told everyone. Everyone at this camp talked ten decibels louder then they needed to.

I got up and walked over to the lodge with the rest of the kids.

Man, there's a lot of kids at this camp. Seriously, where were we all going to stay?

We were supposed to walk in a line but instead we walked in clumps. I saw a big wooden building up ahead. Some kids walked straight into the building, but most had to wait outside. Luckily I was near the front so I didn't have to wait in the long line. I walked inside with a little more than a dozen kids.

"Name?" some grumpy old man at the desk muttered.

"Julian Jimskipper" I said, "I think my mom already filled out my forms."

"Julian... Julian... it looks like you're missing the

B3 addendum. Just fill out these papers," he grumbled. I walked up and read the stack he handed me.

I cleared my throat, "Do you uh, have a pen?" I asked sheepishly. He handed me one. They were basic questions like "what's your birthday?" and "have you been sick in the last twenty-four hours." I finished filling out the missing details on the forms and began to walk away.

"Hey there, homie! Waz new?" the kid from before said to me.

"Um, hey there back at you. Not much," I said. I walked out of the building trying to avoid any more conversation. *What's the deal with that weird accent?*

"Hey kid, do you know what campsite you're going to?" A counselor who's name tag read John asked.

"Um, no."

"What's your name then, kiddo?" he asked me cheerily.

"Julian Jimskipper." He read a paper on a clipboard. "Hmmm... ah! Julian, you are in the Sleepy Hollow campsite." He smiled.

"Thanks. I already knew that." I thought he would do something useful like tell me where the camp site was instead of pointing down the road. I walked down a dirt trail and read some of the signs.

Lumberjack Woods, Medical Center, Dining Hall, Beach, Mount Daisy.

I wondered what some of these places were. I kept walking and reading until I found Sleepy Hollow which was in between the ropes course and archery grounds. I walked toward the campsite. *Seems like some fun stuff here.* For a second I allowed myself to be excited. I may be one of the lucky ones who gets a tent all to themselves I thought. I headed towards the green tent where I had dumped my stuff earlier.

Oh no.

I hadn't noticed before, but there were people's names on pieces of paper taped to the flaps of the tents. I was sharing the tent with someone named Zachary.

Maybe Zachary isn't going to show up I thought hopefully. I didn't have much to do, so I tried to unpack more of my stuff. After I finished laying things out exactly as I wanted them, I opened the tent flaps again and saw a group of people around the campfire. The tents were in kind of a circle and in the middle was a campfire and some gazebo. I walked to the center of the circle toward the fire.

One of the counselors was announcing something. "Okay! We're going to start our opening ceremony campfire!" Then he took out a lighter and lit the wood pile below his feet. He brought out some marshmallows and stuff for s'mores. It seemed a bit early for a campfire, but I guess it was almost evening now.

There were two groups of kids. One was around the campfire eating s'mores and the other was talking by the trees. The group by the campfire looked like a sack of potatoes. I saw the "Z" kid eating five marshmallows out of a half-empty plastic bag.

Ugh, what a pig... who eats like that? I decided to take my chances with the Tree Kids and walked over to them.

They were telling a story about a kid named Mikey who had gone to this camp fifty years ago. Apparently Mikey had gone insane and kidnapped kids.

"They say they never found Mikey ever again!" the oldest kid said in a gravelly voice.

"I heard that Mikey lives in the sewer system under the camp!" said another.

"There is no sewer under the camp! He lives in an abandoned military base underground!" said a third.

I was not buying any of this nonsense, but some

of the younger kids looked scared so I thought it would be fun to toss in some more.

"I heard he throws you into a pit of quicksand and watches you sink!" I added.

"Oh yeah! And he tosses dynamite into the quicksand too!" some kid in a black beanie added. I thought that sounded kind of stupid, and the younger kids must have thought so too because they looked less panicky.

Then one kid went completely pale and wheezed out, "I need my inhaler!" The boy then proceeded to pass out on the ground. I felt kind of sorry for taking it a little too far on that one so I kind of just snuck away and let everyone else deal with that situation. I looked back and saw a camp counselor helping the kid that passed out.

He'll be fine.

I decided to call it a night. I walked over to the campfire for a s'more on the way back to my tent. That's when the "Z" kid saw me coming and frantically grabbed the bag of marshmallows and ran off to god knows where.

I'm in a camp with a bunch of lunatics. I walked over into the woods to go to my tent and opened the flap, hoping to crawl into my bed.

"Waz up?"

Just my luck! I was roommates with this fat sack of potatoes "Z" kid, but on the bright side he was willing to share the marshmallows.

"Thanks!" I said as he offered the bag. I took the fluffy white piece of goodness with a nod.

"No problemz, broski. I alwayz goch your back," he said. I nodded again and hoped it was the right thing to do.

The tent seemed a bit smaller with all of my roommate's stuff jammed in here.

"Hey, home hog, what do youz thinks aboutz that, uh, Mikey story?" he asked.

I laughed, "Crazy right? Who would believe that?"

He looked at me like I said something wrong. "Juz keep your eyes peeled and youz will be fine." He turned around and went to sleep. I didn't like how he did that. It was unsettling.

There couldn't be a guy named Mikey who goes around kidnapping kids, right?

I was having nightmares about falling into quicksand, exactly what I'd told those kids Mikey did to people. The sights and sound were so real I was starting to panic. I felt myself gasping for air. I thought I was a goner, but then I woke up suddenly.

I heard a loud noise that sounded like a bear was dying, but it was just the "Z" kid waking up.

"Oh my god! I needz meself a Big Mac!" he said yawning.

I don't know if you've ever woken up to the sound of someone begging for a McDonald's burger before, but let me tell you, it was a little odd.

"Hey, home hog. Youz gotz any Macs?" he asked me.

I looked at him blankly. "Umm, no." Could he tell that I was sweating and flustered?

He looked like he'd just been stabbed in the chest and groaned. "Oh, why!?" Then kind of just fell out of the tent.

I got dressed quickly and stepped out of my tent after him. It was about 6:30 a.m. and the air was still cool. Leaves and twigs crunched beneath my feet, which was weird because it wasn't even fall. The smell of burning wood was still in the air even though last night's campfire had clearly burned out. I really liked that smell—it reminded me of camping with my family when I was younger. The campsite had a few picnic tables set up, and I saw "Z" sitting at one. I sat down next to him and said, "Hey."

He didn't respond, so I continued, "We didn't really talk last night. My name's Julian, by the way. You must be Zachary?"

He looked at me and said, "Peoplez call me Zack." Huh. And here I was calling him "Z" all the time. Some names just seem to fit. I asked what he was doing.

"Have youz ever played some blackjack?" he asked. He shuffled a deck of cards and split it in two. He shuffled the deck with enough speed that I could tell he had plenty of practice.

"No, but I'll play a quick match." I told him. He smiled and dealt me some cards and we started playing.

"So, you like cards?" I asked him.

He nodded. "My dad taught me how to play a lot of card games. Wez don't really have a lot in common, but cardz is our favorite thing to do at home!"

I was surprised by that. "Huh, how about your mom?" I was curious to know if she was into the cards thing too.

Maybe they're professional gamblers. I'd watched TV shows where people just played cards for money. Talk about an easy job.

"Nah, home hogz. She just workz at her hardware store."

I looked down at my cards.

"Looks like a bust, broski!" he said. "Dealer wins!" In one sweeping motion on the table he collected my cards.

I got bored of blackjack. "Hey do you wanna come with me to get some bug spray from the Trading Post?"

"Yeah sure, broski." We went down a path made of rocks and dirt. It was well worn. Surprisingly, the

Trading Post was really close to the Sleepy Hollow site. I was pretty happy about that.

We walked off the path and across a dirt road—wide enough to barely fit two vehicles. There were kids biking up the road and others just hanging about.

"Have you heard of that mud pitz thing thaz be happening next week?"

I lifted my head up. "What's a mud pit."

"Itz like thiz hole in the ground with mud in it and youz just jump in. You know, like a mud pool!"

"That sounds kind of gross."

"I heard it takez a whole week to prepare it," Z rambled. We walked up the couple of wooden stairs and into the Trading Post. As we entered, the little bell on top of the door jingled in a kind of nice little melody. "Letz grab some candy barz dude."

"No, I just need some bug spray."

"I'm gonna get mez a KitKat," Z said, his eyes going wide with excitement. We paid for our stuff at the cash register.

We left the post and as we were walking down the road, we saw a group of kids huddled and eating a pack of Skittles. Candy wasn't allowed before breakfast, so they were clearly sneaking it. Z should get along with them just fine.

I should introduce myself.

"Hi there! My name is Julian. Mind if I have one?" I asked them as I approached. They looked at me and laughed and then proceeded to hand me an empty wrapper. I ground my teeth and rolled my eyes. Real friendly. Z just stood there with a smirk on his face.

I know I'm supposed to be more outgoing, but people make it so hard.

"I got nothing, Z. What do you want to do?"

Z just looked at me blankly with his mouth full of candy.

We saw a kid walking down a gravel path, so we decided to follow him since neither of us had an idea of what we were supposed to be doing now. Maybe we should have stayed at the site and left with the group. I wondered if I should say something to Z, but I was really bad at small talk. The longer that we walked together, the more awkward it became.

The gravel path actually felt interesting to walk on.

Not a lot of gravel walkways back home. I really started to notice the trail and my surroundings. It was pretty and very calming. Life back home had gotten so crazy.

With Dad moving out, people coming and going,

furniture being removed and changed, nothing seemed peaceful. At home the stress was starting to get to me, but here, it felt different. There was a beautiful pond in the middle of the camp with navy blue water and lots of plants. You could see the shimmering morning sun in the reflection of the waves on the water, which looked cold as the sun burned away the morning fog. We saw monarch butterflies fluttering by the trees and an eagle soared overhead. Z and I were walking so slow we lost sight of the kid we were following. *Oh well.* It didn't matter.

"Alright, alright. One at a time! Come on guys!" I heard a camp director say.

I should have seen it before, but I finally noticed a big white tent that looked like something from a circus. It had a wooden sign in front of it, reading "Dining Hall" carved in curvy letters. Kids were lining up to get orange juice, cereal, eggs, sausages, and bacon. My mouth watered at the bacon still sizzling in the pan. The eggs looked good—nice and yellow and really fresh. The sausages smelled amazing, and it all looked really appetizing. My stomach growled.

Z and I got in line and filled our plates. *This might not be such a bad two weeks.*

As I looked around to find a place for us to sit, I

noticed a torn poster on the wall. It looked just like the one I saw when I'd arrived that read, "Goodie, you're here!" Except this one, ripped up, read, "die, you." Then I remembered what Z had said last night about Mikey.

Just keep your eyes peeled and you'll be fine.

I shuddered at the thought and tried to shake it off. The next thing I knew, I was sitting in front of a bowl of Crunchy O's and some eggs. Z had already squeezed himself in at the table and was elbows-deep in his breakfast. I ended up sitting next to one of the kids from last night that had been talking about the boy Mikey, the one with the black beanie. He had bushy eyebrows and a crooked nose. *Okay, Julian. Let's try to engage some people again. You can't make friends unless you put yourself out there—just like Dad always says. What's the worst that can happen?*

"Hey," I said.

"What?" he asked.

"My name's Julian. How's it going?"

He looked at me with a confused expression and said, "Not bad I guess. What about you?"

"Pretty good," I lied. I hadn't slept much last night. I kept having nightmares about falling into quicksand.

"Good morning, campers! Today we're going to

be having the great canoe race!" one of the camp counselors announced. It was the one who had escorted me from the parking lot. What was his name? A canoe race sounded kind of fun.

"If you would like to join, you'll need to go through the swim test first. Please head on over to the beach by Mikey's Pond!"

My blood went cold and I got goosebumps. *Mikey's Pond? Like the supposedly insane kid? No, no. Mike is a very common name it's probably nothing.*

As I cleared my breakfast tray, I casually asked a camp counselor why they called it that. "The pond was named after a really nice camper named Mikey. He was here the first year of operation! It's too bad he never came back. Parts of the camp were named from the campers that were here on the camp's first year of fun," the counselor said. I started to put two and two together.

Is it the same kid? Who was Mikey? Did he die? Why didn't he come back?

I shook my head. *Mikey is a pretty common name. Shouldn't read that much into it.* I went back to my tent to change into my swimsuit. A long-sleeved rash guard was folded into my swim trunks.

Mom's looking out for me again. I guess I should wear it.

The last time I didn't wear my rash guard, I burned so bad I had to miss two days of school. It was bad, the kind that blistered and was impossibly sore to the touch. I definitely don't want a repeat of that experience.

There were about a dozen of us that met up at the beach for the required swim test. We were called into the water to perform a front stroke and a backstroke. This seemed easy enough. I was a pretty decent swimmer. We were then supposed to float for two whole minutes. I had no problem in the water if I'm moving, but for some reason my body just didn't want to float. "All you have to do is relax," my parents always told me. But I guess I wasn't relaxed, because I always felt like I was sinking to the bottom when I tried to float.

By some miracle, I actually made it the two minutes and passed the test. There were a couple of boys that failed and weren't allowed in a canoe. I speed walked over to the dock to get my canoe. The sand was cold, so I moved quickly. I always thought it was weird how sand could either be really cold or really hot. Then I felt a big SMACK! A canoe paddle had smacked me in the face, and I fell to the ground.

What the heck?!?

"Oopz, sorry about that, home hog," Z said.

Seriously?!

A counselor came over and checked me out. I didn't black out or anything, but I shook my head to regain my focus. My face stung a bit and I was sure it was turning red. I hoped the counselor wasn't going to tell me to sit this one out. I got to my feet and managed to walk with him over to the sandy beach. After getting cleared by the counselor, I saw that all the good boats had been taken. The only one left was a crusty old canoe with chipped paint and I even saw a small fish in it. How was this canoe even fit to be at the camp?

As everyone was lined up and prepared to launch, I scrambled to get my canoe into the water. Then I looked for a paddle and eventually settled on a stick that was kind of flat that was adrift by the shore. I grabbed a life vest, but the strap was set to someone who was clearly super huge and way too big for me. As I was fidgeting with the straps on the vest, a counselor called out, "Three! Two! One! Go!"

Then all the canoes went into the water, splashing and splashing with kids screaming, yelling, and cheering. *Whatever. I'll just throw the vest over my head and not bother with the strap. I can swim.*

My canoe was moving okay at first, which I was impressed by because I didn't even have a real paddle, but then it started to slow down. It was then that I noticed a red sticker with some writing, "DO NOT USE—WILL SINK!"

In my rush to get in a canoe, I had missed a really obvious warning sign. My boat was suddenly filling with water, first slowly, then faster and faster!

"Help!" I shouted. I was frantically trying to adjust the strap on my life jacket. I couldn't pull it through the plastic thingy. It was stuck! I started breathing hard. I was panicking. My canoe was halfway submerged in the pond.

"Help! My canoe's gonna sink!" I shouted again. No one stopped because they were too distracted by the race, which was loud. Really loud. Then, the largest fish I had ever seen jumped out of the water and onto my boat.

"AAAH!" I fell down on my face. The fish was having a spaz attack on the side of my boat—that was sinking! Then I heard a whistle blow and people shouting, and I realized they were finally coming to save me. BLOP! My boat had completely submerged into the black water.

The fish swam off somewhere and then I saw a motorboat coming my way with a lifeguard in it. My life jacket floated up over my head now as it hadn't been strapped down. I knew the lifeguard was gonna say something about that.

"Kid! Come up! Get on!" the lifeguard was shouting at me. He looked angry, staring at first my life vest and then at me. I was still breathing hard. The water was so dark. I grabbed onto the rescue boat. It was then that I felt something touch my leg. Was it a fish? Was it seaweed tangling around my leg? The water felt heavy against my chest. I screamed, "Mikey!"

Then I passed out.

WHEN I WOKE UP, I was in my tent and it was nighttime. I looked over to my right and saw Z snoring. I put my head down on my pillow.

How long was I out? I must have been unconscious for a while. I could hear an owl hooting in the background, along with some crickets to help with the backup vocals to the owl's tired song.

I put my head back onto my pillow and tried to fall asleep but I couldn't stop thinking about how I'd almost drowned. How many of the other campers had seen it? I knew they must have called my mom and told her about it. I felt a wave of embarrassment come over me. *Great, something else for her to be worrying about.* I saw flashes of water rushing into my boat, felt myself panicking to blow up my life jacket, and heard myself yelling for help but no one hearing me.

What will the other kids think of me now?

I fell back asleep eventually, but before I fell asleep I looked outside the small plastic window of my tent. I could see trees, stars, tall grass, and the torn poster hanging on the tall oak tree that read, "die, you."

"Ugh, what's that smell?" Z asked from under the blankets. I looked up and smelled something awful. I looked out of the clear plastic tent window and saw a skunk. *Oh no.* I thought. I tried breathing through my mouth. You couldn't escape the smell. A skunk had sprayed just downwind of our tent. Everyone was complaining about the skunk smell. I was thankful to have the distraction and was hoping nobody would say anything about what happened on the lake yesterday.

Today was weaponry day. We would get to use swords, bows and arrows, and throwing tomahawks. "Hey, home hog. You ready for some swordz?" Z asked.

I shrugged. I put on some clean clothes and got

out of the tent. It was kind of warm today, which was a nice change from the recent weather we had been having. The sun was actually shining for once, and to be honest I had kind of forgotten what it looked like. I wished I lived in a sunny state like Florida or California. Instead I was here in New England and weather was just... weird. My dad was always saying "If you don't like the weather in New England, just wait five minutes. It'll change." Dads are so corny sometimes. I was going to miss that around the house though. It was weird the things you missed when your life changed.

At least now birds were chirping their morning tune. I was starving, I needed some breakfast. *I hope this smell doesn't attach to me.*

"Hey sir, umm what time do we go to breakfast?" I asked one of the camp counselors. The counselor looked at his clipboard and scrunched up his nose.

"Ugh, what's that smell?" he asked waving his hand.

"What smell?" I said trying to shrug it off.

"Hey aren't you that kid that the, uh, trouble, with the canoe yesterday?" He asked how I was feeling and said he had come to check on me a couple of times while I was still passed out. After giving me a lecture about boat safety and reprimanding me for not properly fastening my life vest, he finally told me it was time for breakfast. "So you'd better get a move on," he chuckled.

Before breakfast, we did roll call. I had missed dinner the day before, so I was really hungry and just wanted to get roll call over with quickly. Our campsite had ten boys, yet only nine showed up for the call. At first, the counselors thought one of our campers was still sleeping. It had been known to happen, but after checking tents at Sleepy Hollow nothing had turned up. The rest of our patrol was allowed to head to breakfast while the remaining counselors went about a more complete search of Camp Golden Hills.

One of the campers went missing? What does that even mean?

Everyone started to jump to all kinds of conclusions and kids were spreading all kinds of rumors about what happened to the missing kid—and those rumors were spreading through the camp like wildfire.

"I bet he ran away because he was scared!" said one.

"No, he was abducted by aliens!" laughed another.

"Or he was kidnapped by Mikey!" said one boy

in an exaggerated spooky voice. I rolled my eyes at the last one. Sure, I may have almost drowned at the thought of Mikey, but at that time I was hysterical and panicked, so it didn't count.

I got some bacon, eggs, and a glass of orange juice. The usual. I wanted some coffee but they didn't have any. I hadn't liked coffee until recently when I'd asked my dad if I could have a sip of his Starbucks. I bit into some bacon. *What did happen to that kid this morning?* You could tell the counselors did not like all the commotion that came with a missing camper. I saw at least a half dozen counselors get on four-wheelers and ride out along the trail. Probably to look for the camper. The couple of adults left stood up.

"Attention, campers! It's time to get ready for weaponry day! Make sure to sign up for the activity you would like to do," announced one of the lead counselors.

There were many things to sign up for; there was one for bows and arrows. *That sounds cool.* There was knife and tomahawk throwing and then there was darts, which sounded kind of bland to me—even the counselor who was operating that station looked like he didn't want to be there.

I got up out of my seat to get a spot with bows

and arrows. From the signup sheet I could see there was only one spot left in the roster.

"Move it, home hog!" said a familiar voice. I fell to the ground as Z shoved me. *C'mon! This kid's arms are too short to even hold a bow!* I was upset because that was the only thing I had really wanted to do today. When I was little, my dad would take me to an archery class and taught me to shoot targets. It was really cool because some of the targets moved. I was annoyed that no counselor saw me get shoved by Z and that I had to pick a different station. I headed over to knife throwing.

"Hey, kiddo! Ready to have some double-edged fun?" the counselor running the booth asked.

"I guess so." I didn't really want to have some "double-edged fun." I wanted to have some... *Bow and arrow fun? That sounds stupid, but I'd still rather use the bow and arrows.*

They handed us some gloves so we wouldn't cut our hands. The knife throwing event was over by the beach where I'd lost my canoe the day before. I peeked over to see if there was any trace of the canoe. Nothing. I tried to squint to see more but then I was interrupted by the counselor.

"Okay, kids! Put on your safety gloves and get ready to throw your knife at these targets! It's not too difficult, really. It just takes practice. Like this. Here watch," said the counselor. He went through the rules first, pointing out the dos and don'ts and then showed us how to safely throw the knife and to make sure not to throw it in random directions. Knives were always supposed to be facing down-range.

I was first in line. I went to pick a pair of gloves and they were all way too big for my skinny hands. I asked the counselor if there were any smaller gloves but of course he said no. *Can't anything in my life just work out the way it's supposed to?*

I picked up my knife with my big gloves and aimed the double-edged weapon in my hand for the paper bullseye about twenty-five feet away.

I took a deep breath and threw the knife toward the target. End over end it spun, the metal gleaming as it caught the sunlight. I imagined it landing right in the center of the bullseye. I wish it had been that easy. Nope. What really happened was that I lost control of the knife due to my oversized gloves. The knife released too early and it went flying into the air!

Someone saw what happened and yelled, "Run! It's raining knives!" The knife somehow landed in a large pine tree. A few kids started to panic and in all the commotion someone had tripped and badly hurt his arm.

I clenched my teeth, knowing I was in some hot water now. It really was an accident. I had even asked for a smaller pair of gloves.

The boy was screaming, "Help! I think I broke my arm!" Everyone circled around him as he rocked back and forth on the ground. Another counselor from the bows and arrows station came running over.

The older counselor took a look at his arm. He gently felt around the area, causing more yelps from the kid then said, "I don't think it's broken, but it could be bruised or a mild sprain." The boy ended up with a sling. A pink sling because that was apparently the only color they had. So I had to deal with dirty looks from this kid with a hot-pink sling.

Just like back at home, rumors spread fast around the camp. My parent's divorce was like front page news barely moments after they told me about it. *Why should it be any different here?* By the time I got to the dining hall all eyes were on me. *Why can't I go unnoticed for once?* I couldn't even concentrate on my lunch when everyone was asking me how I broke the boy's arm.

Ugh, it's not broken!

"Hey, home hog! How'd youz break that kiddoz arm?" asked Z as he sat down next to me.

"I didn't break his arm! He sprained it by tripping over a root!"

Z chuckled, "Okay, home hog, whatever youz say!" Nobody at the camp seemed overly friendly to start and now I knew I was gonna get it.

The kid with the sling saw me at lunch and the dirty looks continued. I tried to casually keep an eye on him as I saw him talking to a group of kids. Yup, I knew when someone was plotting something. It looked like he decided to start a riot and miscellaneous food items were soon airborne. In the chaos I saw the kid coming toward me.

He's going to try and sprain my arm for payback!

All eyes shifted to the kid with the hot-pink sling as he shouted. "Charge!"

Everyone was up out of their seats and making quite the mess. I got up quickly from my table and ran out of the white tent as fast as I could. I saw some counselors running behind us to try and catch the kids. One thing most people didn't realize about me on first glance is that I was really fast. I sprinted through the trees to the Trading Post, which was basically a gift shop and convenience store. I ran up the stairs, through the jingling belled door, and hid behind a rack full of gummy worms and gummy bears.

The Trading Post was empty except for the cashier. There was some faint music playing on a weak old speaker, and I figured it was a good place to just hang out and hide for a bit. Lay low. I wasn't planning on staying in there forever, but I was right in front of the heater and it was nice and warm. I crouched behind the shelf and sat down with a bag of gummy worms. This was my life. Something bad happened, something good happened. Rinse. Repeat. Half the time I really wanted people to leave me alone and the rest I wished I had friends who understood me. It felt like I was sitting by the heater forever, lost in my thoughts. With all of the excitement and the warm spot, I fell asleep.

I woke up to the cashier trying to kick me out because it was closing time. The Trading Post closed after dinner. That was when it hit me. *I fell asleep in here!*

"Oh, I'm sorry sir. I, uh I'll just see myself out!" I said as I got up and paid for my snack. I was patting down my shirt because it was all dusty now being behind those shelves. I was still in a bit of a fog as I ran out of the Trading Post and wasn't paying attention as I ran across the path and onto the bridge that crossed a small stream.

There he was, right in my face, the kid with the hot-pink sling! I was running so fast that I had no time to stop. In order to avoid hitting the kid with the hurt arm, I jumped to the side. This wasn't my finest athletic move and as a result, I made the dumb decision of jumping off the side of the bridge and onto a pile of rocks.

"Ow! Oh, that hurts so bad!" I shouted! My leg was stinging really bad.

The hot-pink sling kid, who I later learned was named Gerald, did nothing except laugh and walk away. "Hey you know what they say, Julian! An arm for a leg!"

I wanted to climb up and shove him into the stream, but any movement just made the pain worse. *Wait, how did he know my name?*

I had no choice but to wait right where I was for help to come find me. Right there on a pile of wet slimy rocks. *Z will know that I'm gone and come looking for me!* On second thought, from what I knew of Z, he would probably just put the two cots together and sleep on both. I really should have tried harder to make friends. *What did the counselor say we were doing tomorrow? Art? I really should pay more attention to things.*

My cries for help brought no one. Were those wolves howling in the background? Even though it was getting dark and I was tired, I wasn't sleepy. I chuckled to myself that there was nothing better than sleeping outside when there could be a psycho on the loose, kidnapping campers. I swore I would never take a bed for granted again. Or a shower. I still smelled faintly of skunk. Skunks. Someone had told me once that if a skunk was doing a dance, you had like fifteen seconds to run before they sprayed you. I wonder who that skunk did his dance for. I hope he stayed in with his family tonight because I'd hate to run into him now. But that would have been just my luck.

STARRY FIGHT

It was musty, misty, foggy, and rainy on what would be art day. I woke up in the creek very, very early. My leg was still in pain but the good news was that I could now move my body. I climbed out of the creek using only my arms, which was the hardest thing I had ever done.

I squinted to see anything at all in the fog that morning. I could see that I left a bloodstain on some of the rocks down below. I pulled up my pant leg and saw a huge stain of blood! *Oh no.* My brain went fuzzy and I began to black out at the sight of my own blood. I snapped myself out of it and pulled myself together. My leg was scraped pretty badly.

"Hello?" I called out into nothingness.

I heard a jingling of bells and realized that the

Trading Post must have just opened. I limped over to the brown log building and opened the door.

"Hey, sonny," the man behind the register said with a Golden Hills coffee cup in his hand.

I smiled and said, "Hello!" I hoped he wouldn't see the red stain that had soaked through my jeans. I didn't need any more questions or another trip to the medical facility. Plus that would definitely end with a call to my mom. *Time to play it cool.* I looked around and saw the gummy bear rack that I had hidden behind yesterday and went over to pick up a pack.

"Hey, kiddo. Don't fall asleep over there again, m'kay?" said the cashier. I laughed. He clearly didn't think it was funny though. I pulled out five one dollar bills and two quarters and paid for my gummy worms.

"Thank you," I said in an upbeat voice as I walked out – trying not to limp and draw suspicion. The jingling bell on the door sounded as I left. *I can't show my face up at the campsite, or everyone will just attack me again and I stand no chance with an injured leg. It's not like I'm trying to make enemies.*

As I was sitting on the bridge by the creek eating

my gummy bears, a kid with a ski mask rode up to me on a bicycle. *Now what?*

"Hey there," he said to me.

"Umm, hi, " I responded. He parked his bike at the end of the bridge. I couldn't see his face because of the ski mask.

"Um, who are you?" I asked him.

"C'mon. It's me, home hog!" said a familiar voice.

I smiled and asked, "Sup, Z?"

"Notz much budz." He plopped himself down next to me. "Can I have a worm, brozski?"

I smiled and took out a gummy worm from my pack. "Of course you can." *So even my tent mate wasn't curious where I was last night? Nice. Way to be memorable and stand out, Julian.* Maybe I didn't really want to go unnoticed after all.

Mid-chew, Z said, "Oh my, home hog. Youz got a bad injury on your leg there."

I nodded. "Yeah, it hurts, but I think I'll manage."

He pushed up his silver chrome glasses. "Dontz worry home hog, I gotz a plan—"

Before he could finish his thought, a rock went flying past my face! "Ah!" I screamed. I fell backward and almost went into the creek again.

"Missed!" I heard a familiar voice say, followed by a laugh.

"Charge!" called out the kid with the pink sling.

He had a spear in one hand! "For Gerald!" It sounded like there was an army of people yelling. Okay, maybe it was just a few kids, but I wasn't sticking around.

"Z we gotta get out of here fast!" I shouted.

"Right behind you home hog!" Z said as he picked me up and wrapped me around his neck like a scarf. It wasn't the most comfortable position but it was better than limping around everywhere. We ran over to a pine tree with the letters W.W. carved into it and he set me down. I didn't know what the letters meant. Probably some person's name or something. *Why do I pick out random details at the worst times?*

"Now!" I heard someone say. I wish I hadn't looked up at that moment because just then, two buckets of paint were dumped onto me and Z. One blue and one pink. The paint only got me a little, but poor Z—well, he looked like a kindergarten art project gone wrong.

"Ah! Home hog I needz me a Mac!" Z said.

I shouted back, "Z, you don't need a burger whenever something's wrong!"

Then the two empty paint buckets were dropped

on top of us. CLANG! I felt like my face was dented like a tin can.

Just then the branch that the two kids were standing on snapped! "Woah man!" one shouted. I looked in shock as the kid with the black beanie dropped in front of me.

"Jake, what are you doing?" the other kid said. He had a black hoodie with a smiley face on it with custom embroidery on it with the name "Blake" on the back. The boy Jake got to his feet and smacked Blake on the shoulder. "Hey! That's not fair!" He hit back. Then it just turned into an all-out fight.

There is way too much aggression going on here for a summer camp.

I tried to run away but my leg was handicapping me too much.

"Waitz for me Julian!" Z shouted.

I didn't wait. I had to get out of there immediately.

"No!" Z shouted as I scrambled away. I was limping away as fast as I could.

I saw the art gallery in the distance. That must have been where they'd gotten the paint cans. Everyone was supposed to be there, but they were all-out fighting me instead! Okay, most of them. Some of them? I hadn't really gotten a good look. I hoped no counselors end up asking me about this. I was a horrible witness. I noticed an open window as I approached the art room. I grabbed ahold of the shingles of the shack and hoisted myself through the window.

"Ah!" I yelled as I fell face-first into a replica painting of *Starry Night* by Van Gogh. I looked up and saw all sorts of colors and paints. The art room was well stocked with plenty of supplies. Lots of blank canvases, boxes of crayons, and colored pencils in the corner on a shelf. Of course, no one was here. They were all in the big fight.

The "Starry Fight." I laughed at myself.

I could smell something weird. What was the smell? It smelled like spray paint. KSHHH! "What the—" I shouted. Out of nowhere someone was pointing an aerosol spray can at me. I dodged the attack by rolling around on the floor until I smacked into... you guessed it—buckets of paint!

"Get him!" they shouted.

Then two kids plus Gerald popped out over a table! I did some quick thinking and grabbed a bucket of green paint and threw it right at Gerald. Then his hot-pink sling went green in a matter of seconds!

"Oh my god! What's wrong with you, psycho!" I

said as I got up. My foot was bright blue and green and covered in glue. BAM! I was smacked in the face with a canvas! The two kids with Gerald were hitting me with blank canvases! I scanned the room for something to fight back with.

I saw a shelf with a loose screw and a hammer to my right. I was pinned against the wall so I needed to do something and do something fast. I took the hammer and threw it at the shelf above the two kids. The hammer banged right against the loose screw but still didn't do anything.

"Ow! What the heck is wrong with you!" I yelled as I tried to punch Gerald in the face but his two goons had me pinned by the arms.

Gerald chuckled, "Time to win the war." He said. CREAK. Just at that moment the loose screw on the shelf above gave way and let the shelf came free. It came crashing down on top of the three of them. The shelf didn't hit them, but they were hit by a box of crayons—the 100 pack. They fell to the floor. I grabbed *Starry Night* and used it as a crutch and hobbled out of there.

I heard groaning and moaning from inside the shack, and I looked up. The sun was almost in the middle of the sky now. I looked like a homemade birthday card from a first grader.

"Oh my god, home hog!" I saw Z walking toward me. I waved my hand with *Starry Night*. I felt exhausted, I didn't sleep last night and I'd just gotten covered in paint and glue. My leg was sore, but I was starting to feel numb to the pain. Z and I both agreed it was best to go back to the campsite. When we got back inside of the tent I found a rusty nail under my bed and a rock from outside. *What am I thinking? I can't hang a picture with a nail in a tent.* I did want to hang the picture though, so I needed a new plan. I pulled out the bin from under my cot. Rummaging through it, I found just what I needed: duct tape. I used a ton of it and managed to stick *Starry Night* above my bed. Of course, it was covered in some blue and green paint but it added a touch to the bland green tent with the rips in the top. Z had grabbed a canvas from the art shack and painted a rough painting of a Big Mac.

"Not badz broski" he said to my painting.

"Hey, yours doesn't look bad either," I told him. His Mac didn't look really all that good, but at least he thought it looked good.

Me and Z spent the rest of the day by the camp-fire, singing songs and eating snacks. We didn't see those kids again that day, so I assume they must be over at another campsite. Later on, the kid Jake with the black beanie sat down by us. Z pulled out some hot dogs, (where he'd gotten them I had no idea) and we had some for dinner. They were supposed to be, according to Jake, "Mikey's victims" which I thought was kind of dumb.

It was a corny tradition, but it turned out that I liked singing songs by the campfire! We also learned that Z could play the banjo, but only one song and that was "Cotton Eye Joe." Still, I was impressed.

After we put out the fire with a bucket of water, I headed out to the showers, which was a total nightmare. SNAP! Kids were whipping each other with rat tails and were spraying soap in each other's eyes! I went into the shower at the very far end of the room and closed the curtain. "Here I come!" SNAP! "Ow! My back what the—" SNAP! "Stop that!" I listened to that for a while. *They need more counselors here.*

I tried to wash as quietly as possible. I didn't want to draw any attention to myself. It was funny how things changed. First, I wanted to be in the group and included, then I'd decided I was better off alone. Maybe I should have talked to a therapist like my parents told me. As the water was rinsing away the dirt and paint I started drifting deeper into thought. I did all my best thinking in the shower. I was thinking about my dad talking to me after school ended. He was telling me I was going to be the man of the house now and had to "step up." Honestly, I didn't know if I was that kind of person. I was used to being comfy and laying low. Why had my parents had to mess that up for me? SLIP! The soap went flying out of my hands and under the shower door!

"Hey... Where did that soap come from?" said someone from a neighboring stall. I got nervous, but there was nowhere to run... or was there? I looked around and noticed that there was no roof in the showers, just a tall wall. I climbed to the top of the shower door frame and climbed out of the bathroom with nothing on but a towel. Everything was going as planned until someone threw my bar of soap at my head.

"AH!" I screamed as I fell off the top of the wall right onto my bad leg. Then everyone panicked.

"I thought he was dead!" I heard someone scream. Clearly they missed our campfire sing-along. I used all the chaos as a way to get out unnoticed. I was able to escape mostly clean and mostly unscathed. I looked up at the sky as I was running back to the campsite, and I noticed that there were storm clouds. Who knew what tomorrow was gonna be like, but for now I just needed to get into my tent. The commotion in the distance was dying down.

The counselors were under a tent playing cards at a table. Did they even know what was going on here? *They must not be paid much.*

Laying down on my cot felt so good. What would tomorrow bring? I stared at the roof of my tent, I couldn't sleep. SCRAPE! I sat up in my cot quickly. I looked around. Nothing was there. *That was a really eerie sound.* I lay back down, a little confused. I looked outside and saw the poster "die, you" and got a little nervous. I quietly but frantically tried to find my lantern. SCRAPE! I looked around again as my eyes adjusted to the darkness. I now could see Z rolling around in his bed violently.

"Z?" I said, a little afraid about what was gonna happen next. He rolled quickly out of his bed and onto the floor, wrapped in blankets with a huge thud.

"Z, wake up!" I shouted. I immediately regretted yelling that loud in the middle of the night. Z was rolling on the floor in between our two cots. Then all of a sudden he stopped.

"What happened to me, dudez?"

I started to laugh as Z attempted to untangle himself from the blankets.

"I forgot to takez my sleep medication," Z said.

"You take sleep medication?" I asked.

"Yeah itz just to help my twitchez at night."

"I think that was a little more than twitching," I said, chuckling. We both got back into bed. It was a big day tomorrow. I needed some sleep anyway. My leg was finally starting to feel better and rumor was we were playing capture the flag tomorrow.

CAPTURE THE FLAG

BOOM! Thunder and lightning. There was a huge storm overhead that day. I woke up to a jolt. My head sprung up like a catapult. I didn't want to get out of my tent but I had no choice. I put on a long-sleeved shirt and some sweatpants; I thought that would be better for rain. My mother had given me the camp's suggested packing list. A raincoat was on the list. Of course, I had moaned and groaned at my mother, insisting that I would not need a raincoat. She had everything all laid out and I didn't want to pack it. I knew now it had been a weird argument. There had been no need to make a stand and refuse to bring a raincoat. But I just had to be right. I was wrong and now I was gonna get soaked.

I walked over to the picnic tables in the corner of

the campsite. Z was sitting on one, shivering. "Hey, home hog, wanna join?" he shouted to me. I saw he was playing cards with some kid in a Hawaiian shirt and Jake. I went wide eyed.

"Woah, woah! What's going on here!" I said with my hands out to defend myself. "He was trying to kill us yesterday Z!"

"Nah, iz cool, home hog! Me and this dude talked it out!" Z said casually. "Turnz out hez don't like thoz guys that attacked youz an me either!" Jake looked up and gave me a smile and wave. *If he's good with Z he might not be all bad.*

They were playing some card games. "You wanna join us?" Jake asked. I remembered that Z was good with cards, but I really wasn't up for it now. "I got to get something first," I replied. I went back over to my tent.

What do I need for capture the flag? I knew it was going to start raining soon so I put on my boots. Maybe I could wear an extra sweatshirt? I really should have taken that rain jacket. I went back outside. *I wonder who that other kid with Z was..*

"Attention campers!" a camp counselor yelled. "We do have some bad weather today so we—" CRACK! Lightning hit a tree not too far from us. You could almost feel how close it was. That tree must have fallen down. "Ahem! Even though we appear to have bad weather, we will still play a game of capture the flag!" said the counselor. "The doppler radar says that it should pass and we should only have scattered showers. This should be the worst of it."

You have got to be kidding me. Nobody seemed happy. "Why?" Some person asked.

"Well we need to have a certain number of games to win the—" He stopped. "Never mind. Please line up by height so we can put you in your groups. Shortest to tallest!" I was somewhere in the middle, and was placed with the medium height kids.

"Let's count off by fours. Okay, here we go. Group one, group two, group three, group four," said the counselor.

I was put into group three, which included me, Z, Jake, and that other kid I'd not talked to before. He was wearing a Hawaiian shirt and long khakis with a pair of leopard print glasses. The glasses looked like something my mom would wear, but they were broken at the hinge so he had some leopard print duct tape messily taped to the frames.

"Hey, bro. What's up?" I asked him with my fist out for a fist bump.

"I'm actually not doing very excellent at this point in time," he responded in a high-pitched voice.

"Iz don't thinkz he likz peoples very much bros-ki," Z whispered to me very loudly. I never could understand why people couldn't just whisper normally, but whatever. I looked over to my right and I saw Jake wringing out his black beanie, which now had some bright colored paint stained into it. *I don't know if I should trust this guy.*

"Alright, campers. Teams are sorted, so let's go have some breakfast and then we'll get started!" We sprinted over to the breakfast tent to have some food. I scooped up a big plate of eggs. I was really craving scrambled eggs this morning, and they had really good scrambled eggs at camp. Nice and fluffy. I took an extra spoonful.

"Hey, kiddo, what do ya think of the capture the flag game?" Jake asked me. I still can't believe the camp counselor that sorted us had put Jake in my group. Camp Counselor Bill had a little talk with a few of us about what went on yesterday. He said it was time to act our age and we were going to work on teambuilding.

"Oh I can't wait. It's gonna be aweso—" I started to say.

"Attention, everyone at Golden Hills summer

camp! We have an important announcement!"
Everyone started murmuring to each other. "We
understand you guys have become great friends! But
you want to keep your friends close and your
enemies closer! Slight change of plans. We're going
to make this nice and simple and split the camp into
just two teams! Team Blue and Team Red!" Everybody got upset at that and some people started
throwing food at the camp director. *Yup. Teambuilding. Sure.*

"Attention!" a camp counselor said, "My name
is Bill, and I'm going to be the captain of Team
Blue. I will make sure we wi—" Just then someone
else got on a microphone. "I will be Team Red's
director! I'm Counselor Rick, and it's Red or dead!
Team Red will be the Hickory, Winnipeg, and Kiki-
waka campsites." Bill butted in on the mic. "Team
Blue will be Winnoxit, Hemlock, and Sleepy
Hollow." Oh no! Everybody in those campsites
hated me.

"Guess we're on Blue Team!" Jake announced.
Z, Jake and I high-fived and the new kid just smiled
in approval. We went back to the campsite to make a
team flag. We got a blue shirt and cut off a piece of it
to make a blue rectangle. Then we signed our names
all over it. "Julian, Zack, Jake, and Brain."

"Wait, hold on, your name is Brain?" we asked the new kid.

"No. It's Brian," he said.

"You wrote Brain," Jake told him.

Trying to not attract attention, he responded, "No, it's pronounced Brian but it's spelled B-R-A-I-N. Brian!"

"Broski... Thaz be spellin brain," Z said.

"I know how my name is spelled. I'm not some insignificant pawn!" he screamed, his voice cracking. We looked at each other.

"Whatever, Brain," Jake chuckled.

"It's Brian!" Brain yelled back.

"Geez, calm down," I told him.

We took our flag, which kind of looked like a rag now as it was getting wetter by the minute. Jake climbed up a high tree and hid it where no one would find it. We stood on each other's shoulders to get it high up enough and in a good spot where we thought nobody could reach it. "Okay, guys. So we need a plan," I said.

We huddled around each other, except for Brain who said, "I'm not coming near you sweating beastly creatures!" I rolled my eyes.

We decided we should stay together because there was safety in numbers. "We should go down to the dock because it's near most of the Red Team's campsites," I told them. We headed toward the dock (the one where I almost had drowned). It was raining pretty hard. How did the counselors think this was a good idea?

As we walked toward the dock area, we commented on how flooded and muddy the camp was getting. "AAAAH! I STEPPED ON A SQUIRREL!" Z screamed. We were on a hill that was becoming really muddy and squishy and Z slipped and rolled down the hill. "AAAAAAH!" Z screamed as he tumbled down the gravel path.

"Dude he's heading right toward the dock!" Jake yelled. Sure enough, Jake was right. Z was heading toward the beach. "No!" I screamed as I ran down. CRACK! A bolt of lightning struck and it felt like it was right on us. It wasn't really all that close, but the noise scared me right out of my skin. I turned around a saw that it was a giant pine tree that got struck by the lightning. The tree was uphill and was the sickest looking tree I've ever seen. Most of its branches were dead with just the top of the tree with any green. We could see the tree lean to one side and start to split right at its base. This thing fell as if in slow motion but made a resounding thud as it crashed to the earth. Was it rolling down the hill?

"Impossible," I said out loud. The tree had hit the ground and started to roll straight for us. Brain jumped forward and started to tumble downhill. It figured that this was the section of the camp that was actually cleared of bushes and trees.

"AH!" Jake yelled, moving out of the tree's path. The dead branches were slowing it down. I kept moving. SPLASH! Z was in the water waving his arms around screaming. I tried to do some quick thinking, but I had no good choices. It was like I was living in one of those "choose your own adventure books." *Turn to page 300 if you want to move out of the way!* I had no choice and I jumped out of the way, but I didn't get far. I just scraped my chin against gravel. I looked up to see if I was safe but then BAM! I was knocked out for the second time this week.

WHEN I WOKE UP, I was in a really comfy bed. Way better than the cots that we slept on in our tents. I looked around me and saw Z, Jake, and Brain in beds like mine.

"Good you're awake!" a nurse said to me. "Would you care for some hot cocoa?"

I saw that Z, Brain, and Jake had a cup of hot chocolate in their hands too. I nodded and smiled.

"Here you go," she said to me.

I took a big sip out of the mug. It wasn't too hot and it wasn't too cold. My mom would call it *warm* cocoa.

I looked outside and could see it was still raining hard.

"They said the rain is supposed to last for a while. We're right in the middle of a big storm. They think it might even be a hurricane," Jake said "Typical weather forecast – that doppler report is never right."

Brain chimed in "Um, incorrect sir, doppler is only really useful for predicting the next hour of weather. What it is actually measuring is the wind speed relative to the radar site. They extrapolate the data and make inferences..."

"Too bad, huh?" Jake quickly said to me trying to get off the subject of weather.

I wiped hot chocolate off my upper lip. "What?" I asked.

"Well, duh. Thanks to your plan to go over to the dock we lost the competition." Jake gave me an unpleasant look and took a long sip of cocoa.

Great now they think that I'm a loser with no

sense of direction. Never mind being attacked by a pine tree!

"Hey guys. We're all glad you're okay," Blue Team Leader Bill said. "Don't look so glum guys." Some more kids were behind him. *The rest of the Blue Team.*

"So! As far as tomorrow goes," he started, "if we work together, we can beat them!" Bill seemed confident that tomorrow was gonna solve everything.

"How?" I asked. "Well, today it seems like we kind of split into friend groups." He gave a dirty look at some of the kids behind him. "Tomorrow it's gonna be hard to do that kind of thing."

"How's that?" Brain asked.

"It's a ropes course tomorrow," he said and walked away. *A ropes course?*

Some of the other Blue Team kids brought get well soon cards they made out of some paper that was meant to be letters to mail home. *I should send a letter home to Mom soon.*

Once everyone cleared out of the room, Bill walked back in. "Hey sport," he said as he came up to me. "You kind of blew it on that last event, but I think you can be a real team leader." I looked him in the eyes and I must have looked stunned. I *was* stunned. What made him think that of me?

"How? M-me? I'm no leader!" I responded.

He put his hand on my shoulder. "Look, to be a leader, you simply need to be willing to make a decision and inspire people to follow. Your plan may not have worked out, but you made one. And you convinced the rest of the team to go along with it. People think leadership is something you're born to, but really all it takes is some practice and a willingness to change. If you want some advice, kiddo, just come and see me." He cracked his knuckles. "Well you better get some rest, I guess. I'll see you at dinner later."

"Umm, the nurse says I'm not gonna be able to leave today. I think they want to keep us overnight," I responded.

He nodded and said, "Ah, probably for the best. Well, make sure to get a good night's sleep because tomorrow we're gonna be doing the ropes course." He left the room.

I fell back into my pillow. I would have to stay here for a while. Jake, Z and Brain came back in. Z smiled at me "Bill told the nurse to let us hang with youz broski!"

Jake immediately hopped into one of the open beds. *There it is* I thought. *Bad stuff happens, then good stuff.*

"Hey, Brain, where are you from?" Jake asked.

"I actually live in Connecticut," he said.

"Why are you all the way over here?" I asked.

"Me and my family are on vacation. We like to go north for our adventures" He said. "This year they wanted to follow the Vermont Cheese trail. I was not at all interested in that. I saw a flyer that talked about Camp Golden Hills so I asked my mom if I could come do this instead."

"Cool, broski," Z added "Do you thinkz your parents will bring some cheese when you seez them?".

"How could I know if they will bring cheese? Maybe? This line of questioning is farcical."

Z rolled his eyes and flipped through some pamphlets. "Hey guyz, theyz be havin' a movie night next week!" Z exclaimed.

"Does it say which movie?" I asked.

"*Shrek* 2 dudez."

"Shrek? Isn't that movie like for kids?" Jake asked.

"No, *Shrek* 2," Z said.

"Is there really a difference?" I said sarcastically.

"Yeah. One's good," Brain said.

"*Shrek* 2 was not a good movie."

"Why do you care?"

"Cuz Jake itz be a good movie!"

"Does it come with snacks?" I asked.

"I'll pass and just read comics in my tent," Brain said.

"Wow, so boring. It's amazing," Jake remarked.

"Hey they do have snax, home hog!"

"Now we're talkin'!" I said excitedly.

"You guys are raving about *Shrek 2*," Jake said flatly.

"I'm just gonna bez there for some Twizzlers, dawg!"

I listened to them discuss the benefits of free snacks and my mind wandered. *How am I going to do a ropes course in the rain?* I decided to let it go. I knew tomorrow was going to be awful, but for now, it was nice to just watch the TV overhead playing *SpongeBob* and drink my hot cocoa.

"I knew I should've stayed in bed today," said Squidward on the TV screen above me. I groaned.

"I wish I could stay in bed today too buddy," I said to the TV. I knew that I was gonna have to leave the nice and comfy medical cabin. I looked over to my right and saw an empty mug of hot cocoa. It was almost as if that was the hourglass indicating how much time I had left. Now it was empty and it was time to go.

I saw that Z was getting out of bed and Brain was already about to leave. Jake rose up from the covers and stretched. We all looked miserable. None of us wanted to leave. To go back to the pouring rain. I certainly didn't want to leave this palace after looking outside. It was raining even harder than before.

"Iz don't want to leave thiz place," I heard Z mumble under his breath.

It was cold this morning. You could see the rain battering down the window panes. I sighed because I knew I was in for a long day.

"Oh my gosh home hog, Iz be soooooo tired," Z groaned.

I could barely see out in the rain. I stepped out of the cabin and saw the huge storm we were in and it still looked bad. You could barely tell if it was morning, afternoon, or the middle of the night. I looked back into the cabin and saw an electric alarm clock sitting on a nightstand next to a bed. It was 7:34 a.m.

BOOM! Lightning lit up the sky. You could hear it so perfectly. *There's no way they're going to let us go on a ropes course!*

"Dude we should just get out of here and go to a hotel or something," Jake said.

"We can't just leave the camp! We would get caught and then we would all be in a predicament!" Brain said. "Besides, we need money!"

"I have plenty of money," Jake said, pulling out a leather wallet from his back pocket. "If Brain doesn't want to go then the three of us can pay for one night and we can get an Uber!"

"Hotels cost a lot of cash. I don't think you can cover three people!" I told him.

Brain finally spoke, "Well, we paid money to be here! Our parents paid money for us to be here! And besides, they wouldn't put us in any real danger!"

Z and Jake stood next to each other. "I'm with Jake, weez gotta getz the heck out of here!"

They spent what seemed like hours arguing about whether we should leave. I was not a fan of listening to the arguing.

"You guys are ridiculous, we've been arguing for hours! Let's go have some lunch!" I said.

"Yeah you guys are just hangry about this," Brain chimed in. We made it to the dining hall and sat down for lunch.

"Today we're supposed to be the last table up to get our food," I said.

"Great." Jake rolled his eyes. "When did we start this?"

"I'm guessing the food fight made them want more rules for meal time," I offered.

They all grumbled.

"Moving on, have you seen that funny video that

was posted a while ago? About the llama trying to wiggle his ears?" I asked.

"What?" Brain asked. "How do you wiggle your ears?"

"Like this!" I started to wiggle my ears.

"What!" Brain exclaimed.

"You can't wiggle your ears?" I asked.

"Well can you do this?" Brain bent his arm backward.

"Eww!" Jake made a face. Z tried to copy Brain but couldn't do it.

"What the heck?" he yelled.

"Do you do anything weird, Z?"

He thought for a moment. "I sometimes twitch at night."

"That's not that weird," Jake said.

"Yes it is. Trust me," I said after having seen Z "twitch" at night. Z shrugged. A lunch lady came over to our table.

"You guys can go up to get your food now," she said. We went up and added cereal and fruit on the trays.

"Brain do the thing with your arm again," Jake asked Brain. I grabbed a banana from the trays and put them on my paper plate. *Hopefully this is ripe.* I noticed it had a decidedly weird greenish color. We sat back down at the table with our food.

"Have you guys ever noticed that there are no girls here?" Brain asked.

"Well it's an all-boy camp," Jake said. "You are just noticing this now?"

"Wait, is it?" I asked.

"I mean, I think so. I haven't seen any girls here," Jake said.

"What? My sister is here, home hog," Z said.

"Wait you have a sister?" I asked.

"Yeah, she lives in the dirt." We all looked at each other, really weirded out.

"What?" I asked.

"She's a mole," Z said happily.

"She can't be your sister," Brain said.

"I mean, she could be adopted," I said.

"It's a mole!" Jake yelled.

"Well Jake she's a *she* not an it," Z said.

"You're kidding Zack."

"Well obviously dudez how did youz all believe me?" he asked, laughing really hard.

We headed back down past the first aid station after we finished lunch and Jake's happiness was starting to fade. The weather was starting to get to him. "We should just jump that wall over there and go to that hotel," Jake said.

We looked to our right and saw a ten-foot tall wall.

"How do you even know if there's gonna be a hotel nearby?" I asked Jake, expecting to stump him.

"My mom passed a Holiday Inn while we were driving here," he told us. He crossed his arms, his mouth turned into a smirk. I didn't want to split up, but whatever I was gonna say was not gonna mean anything to this guy. Jake took off his black beanie and wrung it out. It was still soaking wet.

I didn't want to stand there for all eternity, so I decided to say something. "Well if you're gonna go, then hurry up," I said in a tone my mother would use when she wanted me to pick up my room.

Jake immediately ran over to the ten-foot tall wall and Z ran after him. Jake scaled the wall like a spider monkey.

"AAAAAH!" Z screamed. He grabbed a stone poking out of the wall and then the brick literally broke.

"Oh no!" he screamed as he fell five feet in the air. Z smashed into the grass, leaving a huge imprint in the ground that was soaked and mushy from all the rain. Jake was already over the wall and was no longer visible.

"Oh my gosh, home hog. I needz me a Mac," he said with a whine. I raised my eyebrows. I looked over at Brain who was shaking his head.

"I guess we don't have Jake anymore," Brain pointed out. We took a moment to get Z back to his feet because he was lying face-down in the grass. Maybe it was for the best that our group had fallen apart. The three of us walked away from the wall and Z's imprint. Soon we heard sirens in the background.

"Why do youz think therz be some cops?" Z asked.

"Probably someone breaking the speed limit or something."

I looked up ahead and saw the Sleepy Hollow campsite up ahead of us. The thunder and lightning had stopped again but it was still raining as hard as ever. I still could barely see.

"Hey, guys welcome back," Counselor Rick said to us as we walked into the wet campsite. "Today is the day where you get to go on the most fun obstacle course in the world!"

We all looked at each other.

"The Golden Hills ropes course!" Rick explained.

Nobody looked happy when they said that. *How are they gonna let us do that!? We're gonna get absolutely soaked!* I rolled my eyes.

Brain saw me and said, "It's just rain. It's not really cold out. We'll be fine."

Counselor Rick and Bill had everyone get out their rain gear. Everyone went off to their tents to change. I improvised and figured I'd just wear my swimsuit. I grabbed the Camp Golden Hills baseball cap they'd handed out on our first day, hoping it would keep the rain out of my eyes.

Taking command of the Red Team, Counselor Rick announced, "Alright, kids get into a line! C'mon. One by one! Single file!" We got into a wavy line that looked more like a snake that was moving.

"Brozski, Iz can't believe that we gotz to do this," said Z, who got in line behind me. We began to walk on over through the woods past some roots and some trees and leaves. The sky was a dark grey and looking up meant getting water in your eyes. Up ahead the one thing you could see was a dark tall thing in the distance with hanging swings, ropes, ladders, and nets, and this one thing in the middle so high above the ground it would have to be—

"Attention Campers," Rick yelled. "We are going to have another competition! Who can get through the course faster?!! You will be paired to one obstacle each."

Blue Leader Bill was coming around over to me to assign me to an obstacle. "Alright buddy!" he said to me. "You're gonna go to the rope swing." I looked up at the course and saw two identical ropes hanging from a thin wooden pole that I thought was broken and taped in the middle but it was raining too hard to be sure. He continued with, "You're gonna be competing against... Joey!"

I looked over to my right and saw a tall kid with curly short hair and wearing a Metallica T-Shirt. There was a ladder that lead up to the ropes. The station before the rope swing was the zip line. That's where Z was assigned. He was paired off to compete against some other kid. When Z jumped off of the zip line platform, the zip line kind of bent down and just drooped with Z still on the rope. He was stuck halfway through the line and just hung there begging for a Big Mac.

"Help!" he screamed out as he lost the first event of the competition.

I looked back at what I was supposed to be doing.

"Three, two, one, go!!" announced Red Team Rick.

I climbed up as fast as I could, and Joey was right behind me. I got to the top and my blood was racing through my veins. I was looking up so my baseball cap was useless. Water was pouring into my eyes, but I managed to see two ropes with a knot at the end. I grabbed ahold of the rope and jumped! Joey was a little ahead of me and jumped first. He jumped off of the rope in mid-air and landed onto a platform on the other side.

I tried to do the same thing. However, when I did it, I let go too early and went plummeting below. Thankfully there was a net below to catch you if you fell and I landed smack in the middle of the net. I heard the Red Team cheer and then I heard everyone move onto the next event, not caring that I was tangled up in the net. I felt like I was in a spiderweb and I couldn't get myself untangled.

I tried to move my arms out of the net holes but I was stuck. After about a couple minutes of just moving around in the net, it snapped and then I fell five feet to the ground.

"Woooh!" I heard in the distance. I could see kids holding up some random dude on Blue Team who was wearing a blue ribbon. The Red Team behind them had balled up fists. We won!

"Help!" I shouted at them, but they just walked past me. I sighed and just sat there all bundled up in the rain.

Bill walked over to me with a knife, which did not look too great. "Hey buddy," he said as he cut me free. "We won, how about that?" I smiled too but I felt like I was getting hypothermia from the rain. I looked up and saw the ropes course dripping wet. He finished cutting me free and we walked back to camp together.

"Look sport, I know it's tough but you're gonna pull through in the end," he said.

I shook my head. "No I'm not."

"Hey the next big thing we're gonna do is a hike. Can you do that?" he asked. I nodded yes. "Then the only thing to worry about after that is shelter building," he continued. I told him I had no clue about how to build a shack out of mud or whatever. "Don't worry."

He handed me a flash drive, "Here take this. It has all the info on how to build a good shelter from just a few twigs and leaves," he said. I took it from him. *What am I supposed to do? Plug this into a tree or something?* I looked up at him and was thankful for the kind words and encouragement.

"I'll see you in a couple days," he told me.

"What?" I asked.

"You get to go home for the weekend. You leave tomorrow," he told me as we approached the sign that read Sleepy Hollow. We were back at the campsite. I couldn't believe it had already been a week. I felt like I needed a break. I looked at the flash drive in my hand, which now made more sense. I clenched the little black piece of metal in my hand and said, "I'm ready."

Later that night we had a little campfire outside our tents. It was dark and it was perfect for telling some scary stories. We gathered around the flames, which were impressively large. Some random kid was holding the flashlight close up to his face. "There was once a group of five kids. They walked into the dark woods at night—"

"Why?" Brain interrupted.

"I don't know, be quiet," he said.

"Anyway. They saw a man approaching them. First he was walking, then he was running!" the kid continued. "He pulled out a knife—"

"Woah, woah, woah, where did he get this knife? Did he have it in his pocket? He would have cut himself by putting it in his pocket," Brain said annoyingly.

"Shut up!"

"The man grabbed one of the kids by the hoodie—"

"Wait, they're wearing hoodies now?" The kid stood up quickly and grabbed Brain by the collar of his shirt.

"Be. Quiet."

"Okay uh Iz just gonna mosey on out of here!" Z started to shuffle back to our tent.

"Yeah, me too." I followed him to our tent.

Many hours after the fire had died and everyone had gone to bed, I couldn't sleep. I tossed and turned in my cot. I looked at the floor and saw a sharpie marker. *Hmmm.*

"Hey Z!" I whispered.

He didn't wake up. I took off my blankets. I grabbed the sharpie marker off the ground and looked over at Z, who was snoring away. I crept beside his bed. I uncapped the marker slowly. *This is gonna be funny.* I put the marker tip up near his upper lip and drew a mustache.

SNORT! Z rolled over. I thought he was gonna wake up.

"No, no, I want more cheddar," he mumbled

sleepily. I thought this was funny so I got my clothes on and went outside to Brain and Jake's tent. I opened the tent flaps. Jake was gone so I couldn't do the same to him. I moved to Brain. I gave him a goatee. His eyes opened, which startled me. I fell backward. He blinked a couple of times and went back to sleep. "Okay," I said. I went back into my tent. I couldn't wait to see everyone's reaction in the morning.

My eyes opened and saw Brain and Z hovering over me. "What the heck?" I said. I immediately recognized that I was tied to the cot. I couldn't move my arms.

"Help—"

Brain quickly covered my mouth. Z uncapped a marker and drew whiskers and a little nose on my face. He handed the marker to Brain. He drew a unibrow in between my eyebrows. He gave the marker back to Z.

"Thiz is what you get," he said. Then he drew hearts on my cheeks. Brain untied me. I sprinted out of the tent toward the gross outdoor bathroom to look in the mirror and see what they'd done.

"Oh my god!" I screamed. I turned around and saw them laughing.

"Whoz be laughing now!" Z said, chuckling. I turned on the sink, which was a little rusty, and washed off my face. I could still see the marker all over it. Not good. Then I spied the rubbing alcohol on the sink next to me. *I bet that's how they got it off* I thought to myself. I grabbed the bottle and used it with a cloth. Luckily, the marker then came off pretty easy. I suppose it was fair. I vowed to come up with a better prank next time. I saw people gathering by the trail to leave our campsite. I knew they were getting ready to leave, so I quickly packed up my stuff and went with them.

"Alright! Alright everybody. One at a time!" called out one of the camp counselors as they were trying to make sense of pick-up.

"See you in two days! Miss you! See ya bro!" I heard kids saying to camp mates. None of those things were what I was saying on that Saturday morning. Z had already left with his mom and Jake managed to "escape" from the camp when he'd gone over the wall. There were all kinds of rumors flying around about what happened to him: people were saying Mikey had gotten him, and some kids on Red Team were saying he got recruited, although I wasn't sure to what. I hadn't bothered to tell anyone what had really happened to him. I probably should have. Maybe I still should?

"Julian Jimskipper!" I heard someone yell. I looked around and saw a man in one of those neon-yellow vests with reflective tape on it. Next to him was my mom in her busted up white minivan. Ugh, I hated that car, with its ruined leather seats and the stains everywhere from when I was a little kid. I remembered the one time when I was five years old that I spilled a whole container of chocolate milk, pouring milk onto the floor of the car. She reminded me of that story whenever I would complain about the minivan.

"Hey hun!" I heard my mom yell. I speed walked across the gravely road. The storm from the last couple of days was finally passing over us, but it was still partly cloudy. "How was the first week?" Mom asked me. I thought of all the things that had happened at camp at once. What a mess. Almost drowning, doing a ropes course in torrential rain, bruising my leg, jumping off a bridge, getting attacked with paint cans, almost killing people with knives, and then spraining a kids arm.

"Good!" I lied while pulling off the stupidest smile the world had ever seen. I didn't want her to know I was getting into trouble. She had enough going on herself. I reached over to my right as I grabbed the seat belt and clicked it onto place. Mom wrapped her fingers on the steering wheel. HONK!

"C'mon move it!" my mom screamed at some kids walking across the street.

"Geez, Mom, you don't have to be so aggressive to pedestrians," I said as I slid down my seat so I couldn't be seen by the kids in the crosswalk. My mom put the pedal to the metal and the minivan went from zero to thirty in a matter of seconds. It felt like we were going ninety miles per hour in the rickety van. My mom's fuzzy dice on the rear-view mirror were swaying back and forth violently. She had been acting a little more aggressive to everybody but me ever since she and dad split up. I thought we were going to hit the guard rails when my mom made a swift turn by a wooden sign that read: Golden Hills Summer Camp, Est. 1926.

We zoomed past trees and zipped past rocks. We got onto the highway.

My mom pulled out her phone and set her phone's GPS. "Turn right in five miles," the robotic voice on the phone said.

"I thought I was going to Dad's this weekend," I said.

She didn't look at me. "No, you're going to be with me this weekend. Your father didn't want to drive out here. Being lazy as always." I didn't like when my mom talked liked that about my dad, but I didn't want to upset her or anything. I saw a sign on my right hand side that read FOOD EXIT 76.

"Mom, can we get some food?" I asked her.

"I don't know honey. We're gonna be home soon, and I planned on making your favorite for dinner," she said shaking her head.

"C'mon! Please!" I begged.

"No we're gonna—" she tried to respond.

"Ugh!" I groaned.

"Fine. Fine. I guess you can have a little treat. We'll just get some fast food." She turned on the blinker, pulling into a nearby Taco Bell. We placed our order, and when I reached for my burrito, my arm was exposed and mom looked shocked. She immediately asked me, "What happened to your arm?"

I looked down at my left arm and saw that I had huge bruises and scrapes. "Uh... nothing, I was just, uh... playing capture the flag and uh..." I remembered tumbling down the gravel hill and the tree almost rolling over on top of me and my friends. "I fell and scraped my arm on some gravel!" I said, kind of telling the truth.

I looked for an exit to the conversation but my mom wouldn't let it go, "Geez and your legs are all banged up too! Your hands! Did you get a rope burn?"

I lied, "I... uh... was playing, uh... tug of war?" It sounded more like a question than an answer.

"Is that marker on your face honey?" she said.

"Uh no," I said wiping my face.

"I was worried when they called me from camp. Are you sure everything is going okay?" as she was inspecting me from head to toe. "Ugh is that paint in your hair?!"

CLANG! I remembered the noise that the paint buckets made when they fell on me and Z. "Oh yeah! We painted pictures and stuff on art day! I made this really cool picture and I spilled some paint on myself when I made it! And... I made the painting for you!" I fake smiled.

"Oh that's nice! Can I see it?" she asked.

"Okay!" I said as I ran to my mom's car parked outside the Taco Bell and opened the trunk. I dug through all my stuff from camp. Backpack, sleeping bag, *Starry Night*. I grabbed Van Gogh's painting from the car and made a run back into the restaurant.

"See?" I told my mom. She looked at it for what felt like half an hour but was only like a couple seconds.

Ummm... That's *Starry Night.* Just with bright pink paint splatters on it," she said.

I quickly told my mom, "Well, uh, you can't be great at everything! I guess art isn't my thing."

I felt like an idiot just standing there. I grabbed my burrito and took a final bite that was just a little too big. "SPLORF!" I choked spitting food out all over the table.

"Ugh! C'mon Julian! Look at the table! Seriously!" She reached into her purse and pulled out some baby wipes despite there being no baby in our house and there were napkins sitting right on the table. She wiped up the beans and tortilla that I spit out.

"Let's just get going," my mom said. We exited the restaurant and headed back to the car. I opened the passenger seat door—the one that was always sticky, and climbed in.

About fifteen minutes later, we made it home. I looked at the single-story blue house with the big yard and our birch tree in the front. Our house had a flower garden that me and my mom planted before in the spring. Looking at my house was like looking at an old friend. I smiled walking past the open door and breathed in the air of my house.

"Mmrf," I heard below me.

I looked down and saw our fat cat whose belly touched the floor when he walked. His name was Remmy. He was a grey cat with green eyes. "Aww... hey buddy!" I smiled and picked him up.

"WRAHWR!" he yelled when I picked him up.

"Ugh, he never wants to be picked up," I muttered.

"Well honey, go put your stuff in your room," my mom said. I grabbed my backpack and painting and walked down the hall.

I saw a nail sticking out of the wall with nothing hanging on it. I looked to my left and the right, shrugged and plopped *Starry Night* onto it. It was like if a parrot had actually painted the painting because it had splatters of paint and glue all over it. *Aw man that painting looks a little bent.* But I knew why. I had used the painting as a crutch the day I had hurt my leg. I walked further down my hallway and opened my bedroom door.

Wow.

It was so weird being back in here and instead of the green tents and cots they had at Golden Hills. I plopped my bag down on the ground, then jumped into my bed. I looked up at the Metallica poster I had on the wall. I had gotten that at a live concert a while back. I sighed when I looked at my alarm clock. 5:59 p.m. I sat up and stared at my clock. I liked to watch it turn from 'something fifty-nine" to the next hour. The time shifted to p.m. I was bored so I went downstairs. I went down to my living room. My mom was watching TV. Remmy was sitting next to her on the couch.

"Hey, honey!" she called over to me. I sat down on the couch.

"Oh, no. Jefferson! He's... dead!" the woman on the TV said.

"Ugh, turn on something good. Your shows are boring," I said.

"No it's the season finale—"

"Ugh." I walked away over to the kitchen to get a box of Lucky Charms. I grabbed a bowl and poured in the cereal.

"Meow." I looked up and saw Remmy on the kitchen counter.

"Oh, hey Remmy." I reached out to pet him.

"RAWR!" He scrambled around the counter and knocked over my bowl. CLASH!

"Remmy!" My mom rushed into the kitchen.

"Oh my god, Julian!"

I panicked.

"It's not what it looks—"

I heard the TV in the other room. "Sara loves Derek!"

I slouched down. "Mom, your soap operas are dumb." I cleaned up the mess on the floor and made a new bowl of my favorite cereal. After I finished eating it, I went back up to my room.

Sitting on the bed, I looked over at the backpack leaning against the wall. *The flash drive.* It was almost like it was calling to me but I had to do something else that was more important. Sleep.

When I woke up at noon, the sun was shining. *I guess that's why they call it Sunday.* I went over to my backpack and grabbed the flash drive. I looked around for my laptop. CLICK! I popped it in the side of the laptop. I looked for the file labeled GOLDEN HILLS. I clicked on it and it led me to a video. It looked like something you'd see on *YouTube*.

"Okay so this is how we make a sheltah," an Australian man said on the screen. "Fehst ya find sahm good sticks to build with," it continued to tell me how to make a good shelter. I went into my garage and grabbed up some sticks from the yard. I made a small shelter fit for one person in about ten minutes. I looked at my creation in the gleaming sunlight. *Perfect*. I looked into the house window and saw Remmy in the window. He almost looked like he was impressed! I smiled. I knew I would win this competition. I took my shelter apart and put the sticks into our shed with the firewood.

It was time for dinner. My mom had made another favorite meal for my weekend at home. She made beef stroganoff. Yum. I just wished she wouldn't put so many mushrooms in it. I always picked them out and then she'd reach across and scoop them off my plate. Thankfully she didn't ask too many more questions about camp. After dinner, I made a bowl of ice cream with hot fudge on top. My mom clearly had gone shopping and got me all of my favorites. It was nice to be home.

I plopped myself on my bed in front of the TV and browsed for movies. I eventually came across all five *Home Alone* movies. *Aw yeah!* I put the disk into the DVD player, which was kind of old. We had Netflix on the TV downstairs, but I wanted to stay in my room all day. I spent the evening watching *Home Alone*. I loved those movies. The first one was my favorite. The way the kid hit the robbers in the face with paint cans was too much. *Priceless!* I looked over my shoulder and saw my alarm clock reading 11:24 p.m. *Yikes!*

I felt like I had wasted my day but it had been good to relax. I wanted to get back to camp. As much craziness as there was there, it felt like a mission I had to complete. Sleep would be a time machine to my quest. When I woke up I would be going back to Camp Golden Hills. I turned my TV off and put my empty bowl of ice cream to the side. I grabbed the chain part of my lamp and tugged down, signifying the end of my day.

BEEP BEEP BEEP BEEP! SMACK! I hit my alarm clock right off of my nightstand. I looked out my window, the sun was rising over the horizon. "Ugh," I groaned. I knew I wanted to go to the camp again but in that moment I honestly just wanted to stay in bed.

"C'mon you're gonna be late!" Mom shouted from outside my bedroom door. I got out of bed and grabbed my things. As I was walking out I saw *Starry Night* in the hallway. I grabbed it real quick. I don't know why, but I wanted more decor in my tent while I stayed there for another couple days. I got into the car and buckled in my seat belt. We got there after a slight delay while stopping for gas. I saw the big wooden sign saying Camp Golden Hills. I knew in my head that I was ready, but I didn't feel ready. I saw the line of cars ready to drop of kids.

"Alright honey, have a good time. And this time don't get a million scratches. Come home in one piece," she said as she leaned in to give me a kiss. I rolled my eyes.

"Love you too, Mom," I said. I walked out onto the dead leaves on the ground. I looked at the bright sun in the sky.

"Whatz up, home hog?" I heard behind me.

"Zack!" I exclaimed.

We high-fived, "Whaz new broski?" he asked.

"Nothing much... just that we're gonna dominate the competition!" I said.

He looked at me and frowned. "If we win this thing. The Red Team probably has thiz competition rigged!"

"What?" I said like he was joking. I looked around to see if I could find Jake and Brain. They would know about Red Team cheating if they were. I saw a police car pull up, then I saw Jake get out of it.

"Alright, alright. I'm going, okay! Yeah, I love you too. I heard Jake tell the cop. The officer said something else, let him go, and then drove off.

"What did you just... Did you just say 'I love

you' to the cop?" I asked. Then Jake, Z, and I started chuckling.

"Well, when I ditched camp, the wall that I climbed had a ton of graffiti all over it and the po-po thought I was the one that did it," he said.

"Makes perfect sense to me. Your outfit makes you look like a lower lifeform," said a familiar voice.

"Brain!" Z said.

"As I was saying," Jake continued. "They thought I was the one who did it, so they called my dad to pick me up. But my dad is actually a cop, so he bailed me out again. So my dad was telling me to stay out of trouble this time." He rolled his eyes then looked at Brain. "Wait, what do you mean lower lifeform?"

"Look at you and then look at me!" Brain said.

Brain was wearing a blue Hawaiian shirt with tikis and palm trees on it. Jake was wearing an AC-DC T-shirt, his black beanie, and some sweatpants. Z was wearing a white T-shirt with a hamburger on it. I was wearing a green shirt with some jeans.

"I see a worker at a resort in Hawaii," Jake said to Brain.

I heard a loud buzzing behind me.

"Woah, what's that?" Jake yelled. We turned

around and there were some people in hardhats cutting down a tree with a chainsaw.

"You kids gotta get outta here. We're making way for the new solar farm," one of the guys in hardhats told us.

"Whaz be a solar farm?" Z asked. "Howz you grow solarz?"

"Don't embarrass yourself, they're putting a photovoltaic system over there to provide free electricity for the camp," Brain said, like it was obvious. "You guys never wondered where the lights in the bathroom and the gazebo come from?"

"You guys gotta get out of here!" the hardhat guy yelled over the noise. We ran out of the drop-off area to our campsite and put our stuff down.

"Hey you! You're bunking with me again *Brain*," said a boy that was making fun. Brain looked a little uncomfortable.

"Guess that means we're gonna bunk together again," I told Z. I grabbed the painting and hung it up in our tent. It needed just a little more touch of home, so that would do it. It turns out Z brought his painting of a Big Mac back as well. He even got his framed. Z rolled out his sleeping bag from his backpack. I took out a lantern I had packed. Of course my mom had hid the batteries in a small pouch in my backpack so I couldn't find them at first. Z took out a flashlight and helped me dig through my bag until we found them.

"I should've packed this myself," I muttered under my breath. I pulled out a portable fan and some chips and Z brought out a battery-powered lava lamp.

It looked more like a college dorm than a camp tent, but that made it look more like home or something that you could call home. It was like a little apartment in there. We stepped outside and walked down the trail to the beach to get some fresh air. It wasn't that far from the campsite. We headed over the winding and rocky path by the sand. It was cloudy so there wasn't anybody near the water. I saw Bill, the Blue Team counselor standing over in a clearing.

"What are you doing?" I asked him.

"Huh?" He turned around. "Oh hey there sport." He had a box in front of him with a laptop on it. I looked over onto the ground.

"Uh, what's in that bag?" I asked.

"It's a screen," He said.

"What?"

"What are you guys doing?" asked Counselor Bill. "Did you watch the vid?"

"Yeah."

"Then what are you doing here?" He explained that everyone was gonna be going on the big hike up Mount Daisy after lunch.

We decided to go back up to the dining hall. We got our trays and got some spaghetti and meatballs with a breadstick on the side. We sat down at our usual table.

"So you guys looking forward to the hike coming up?" I asked the guys.

"Not really," Jake said.

"Ya know, I actually hiked the high point of a state," Brain said.

"Really? Which one?" I asked.

"My family went on an east coast vacation. One of the things we did was hike the Rhode Island high point," he said.

"What waz it like?" Z asked.

"We packed up all our gear first. Then it was just a long ride to it. We stopped for some food on the way at a nearby *Arby's*. And then we stopped by this guy's house and walked into his backyard—"

"Wait what?" Jake interrupted.

"That's where the high point was. So we walked deep into this guy's property at least 500 feet into a little clearing and there was a little lump of land a couple feet high. So I stepped on top of it," he finished.

"Thatz it?"

"That's the story!" Brain exclaimed.

"What?" Jake said.

"That can't be the high point," I said.

"Look it up!" he said.

"Wez can't. We're in the woodz!" I just went back to enjoying my lunch while they kept arguing about the high point to Rhode Island.

After lunch we headed down the road where there was transportation that was supposed to take us up to the mountain. We walked over to a rickety old truck that was our designated ride up to the base of Mount Daisy. We sat in the back of the truck and it had a rusty floor and had baseball-sized holes everywhere. I climbed in, sat down on a bench in the truck, and it broke. The metal clanged underneath and left a huge dent.

"These trucks are a living nightmare," Jake said. The truck made rumbling noise which I assumed was the engine. We went down an extremely bumpy road where I thought the truck would flip over and we would die. We laughed the whole ride. How were these trucks legal to be on the road? We managed to survive somehow and after a bumpy ride we made it to the mountain.

Mount Daisy was a small mountain with, as you guessed it, a lot of daisies all over the mountain. In fact it was so small you could race up it, which was actually what we were expected to do.

"Alright guys," Bill told us, "What we're gonna do is race up that mountain and grab that flag up there." Sure enough, if you looked up you could see a purple flag waving in the wind. It was probably meant to mean red and blue combined—because of the purple color. Or maybe that was just its design. I saw Red Team getting ready and stretching. Rick was probably giving them the same pep talk he gave us.

"On your mark! Get set! Go!" Rick and Bill shouted. Both Red Team and Blue Team ran up the side of the mountain which, again, was more of a really big hill. In fact, as I learned later, to meet the height requirement to be called a mountain, they had to put a lot of boulders on top of it to make it taller.

I was running at a steady pace but I was slowing down and running out of breath. Z was panting loudly and his panting oddly sounded both wet and dry at the same time. Brain was also running out of breath. Jake however was full-on sprinting up the trail. Rocks were flying behind him he was running up so fast.

"Woo! That's what I'm talking about!" I shouted. I fell down to my hands and crawled like a spider up the mountain.

"AAAAH!" Z screamed. I looked back to see he was laying on the ground face-down.

I shouted to him, "Zack there's a pile of Big Macs at the top!" He looked up with a dead serious face.

"Moooove," he yelled and then he was pushing Red Team out of the way. He was right next to Jake, who was still running up the mountain. Jake grabbed his black beanie to not let it fall off because the wind was getting strong. Brain's Hawaiian shirt was blowing around as he moved up the trail.

"Kind of windy!" he shouted to me.

"Yeah, no kidding," I replied.

Joey, the kid I had faced on red team for the ropes course, was gaining on Z and Jake. Z was dripping with sweat and looked like, hilariously, a Big Mac. Jake slipped on a patch of rocks and they slid behind him, getting in the way of the Red Team runner.

"Woah!" Joey screamed as he ducked out of the way and slowed down.

"Julian, behind you!" Brain yelled to me. I looked

behind me and some kid was about to pass me. I put my hands down, almost running on all fours to stay in front of the kid.

"Nice!" Brain high-fived me.

We were almost at the summit at this point, but we were still neck and neck with the Red Team. We came out into a mostly flat open field with a ton of daisies everywhere. In the middle of the field was the flag. We sprinted after it and so did the other team. We both grabbed it at the exact same time. Kids were tugging and pulling on the flag. I had a good grip but I couldn't get it to move even a little bit.

Some camp instructor in a golf cart pulled up at the top. "Hold on, hold on. Who got it first?" he asked us.

Some small kid in the back of Blue Team piped up, "Uhh we kind of... tied, sir."

The counselor looked puzzled. "Uhh, that means.. I guess it's a tie," he said.

"But sir! Who does the point for this round go to if it's a tie?" I asked.

"Well, I guess you guys both get points," he replied. It took a while to realize but then we knew it was a good thing.

"Well at least we didn't lose!" I told my buds.

"Yeah... Hey where's the Macs?" Z asked.

"Dude," I said with a smile and chuckled. We both started laughing. It wasn't a win but as long as we didn't lose that meant we were still in the competition.

Later that night, we had the movie night that was rumored to happen. It was *Shrek 2*. Not the greatest movie ever, according to Brain.

"Are you guyz ready for some Shrek!" Z yelled.

"Dude shut up," Jake said.

"Thanks for getting us snacks," I thanked Z.

"Huh? No man thez be for me!" He was holding about the equivalent of a bucket full of candy.

"Dude!"

"What homie?"

Jake stared at the candy in Z's arms. "That can't be healthy."

"Hey if the three of you want to get on over to the movie you better hurry up it starts in a couple minutes," said Brain.

"Guys, let's go get a good spot on the grass." We walked down the path from our campsite over to an opening in a place called "Lumberjack Woods" where there was a movie screen and projector set up.

"Come on, guyz!" Z whispered really loudly. We sat down in the very back of the cluster of kids sitting there. Someone pressed play on a laptop behind the movie screen.

"Man, I can't wait!" Z screamed.

Jake went wide eyed and slapped Z in the face.

"OW!" He shouted.

"Put a sock in it!" Jake quietly yelled at Z.

"Guys, shut up. You're causing a scene." I whispered as some people were starting to look behind and try to figure out what was going on. Z unwrapped some candy, loudly, and shoved it forcefully in his mouth.

"Hewr hum hohg," Z said to me with an Air Head in his mouth. He handed me a pack of Twizzlers. Jake played on his phone.

"What the heck, Jake? We're not supposed to be using phones in camp! Do you want to get it confiscated" I said to him.

"Ugh, fine," he said and put it back in his pocket.

"How do you even have that? I thought you told us they grabbed yours the last time you had it out?" I badgered him.

"I have my ways." Jake smiled. "I mean it's not like there is any signal out here anyway."

The rest of the night was pretty uneventful until the end of the movie. The credits started rolling, then Z started clapping and cheering.

"Stop!" Jake said and threw a candy bar at Z.

"Hey, knock it off you two! Get to your tents!" Rick, the Red Team counselor, yelled.

Everyone kind of shuffled back to their tents. I was ready for a good night's sleep and a little bit of rest. Bill told us there wasn't going to be an official competition event tomorrow. That didn't make me sad.

CHESS AND MUD

I hopped out of bed and threw on my clothes and bolted out of the tent. It was like I had nine coffees in me, but whatever. I couldn't explain where all the energy had come from, but I was glad to have it. I waited for my tent mate to come out. When just about everyone was out there we walked down the dining hall to have our breakfast. I didn't want more eggs and sausages so I just had some orange juice.

"Attention campers!" Bill announced. "Today we will be taking a day off from the competition so the staff can attend to some matters. You are free to do whatever you want. By the way, if you want to go to that mud pit activity that will be happening in around five minutes or so."

"Guess I'll skip breakfast," I said.

"Yeah, I wantz to go too," Z said. Z ran down ahead of me. He must have been really excited for this thing. I went down to the main gravel path. This path was supposed to lead to all the parts of the camp. Sure enough, I saw a sign that said "Mud Pit This Way" up ahead. I followed the sign and took a left that it was pointing me to. I saw a bunch of kids in a line that was longer than I thought it should be. I knew Z was going to be here somewhere. I got in the line that was for going down to the mud pit, I still had no idea of what it was going to be like. I assumed it would be disgusting.

"Man, I hear thiz thingz supposed to be really fun ya know?" Z said from behind me. "Iz been waitin' a whole week!"

I shrugged. "I guess so." I didn't really see the appeal. I noticed the line beginning to move down the gravel path and over to a cleared spot in the forest in the middle of what looked like a swamp. My eyes went wide.

"That's huge!" I told Z. I stared at the huge indent in the ground which contained almost as much mud as an Olympic-sized swimming pool.

"No!" someone screamed as they were pushed in.

"Geronimo!"

"Woohoo!"

"Wait for me!"

People were shouting and causing a general ruckus. I inched closer to the mud thinking about all the bugs and germs in there. I'd gotten dirty plenty of times before, but as I got older, I kind of preferred being clean.

"Get in!" Z screamed then he rammed into me. I wobbled forward and had no other choice than to accept my fate and join the rest of the kids in the mud.

"Ugh," I sputtered. I was up to my waist in it.

"Dude, look out!" I turned around and mud slapped my face.

I saw some chuckling little runt in the back of the pit. I rolled up my sleeves and scooped up a big ball of mud. I chucked the big sticky ball right at his face. His eyes went wide then his face was hit dead on with a ball of brown.

"Nice shot, broski!" I engaged in a fun mudball fight. I seriously had mud coming out of everywhere, but so did everyone else. But the fun wouldn't last long. I really needed to get cleaned off. I hosed off with the rest of the kids and tried to find a dry towel.

I wasn't particularly hungry so I decided to go to the Trading Post and just grab a few snacks. Walking back from the post to my campsite I enjoyed the relative calm of the day. I probably still had mud in my ears, but hopefully that would come out with the next shower. Eating my makeshift lunch, I headed back to my tent. I saw Brain sitting in that little gazebo in the campsite. He was playing chess by himself. He was playing both sides just flipping the board around each turn. He looked at me.

"Hey Julian do you want to play chess?" he asked me. I looked over at him. I knew how and had nothing better to do.

"Sure," I said. He started rearranging the chess pieces on the board. They looked really nice. It was a fancy wood kind.

"Do you want to be whites or blacks?"

I didn't think it really mattered so I just said blacks.

"Okay but the white pieces go first you know," he said.

"I think that going second gives an advantage because you get to see what your opponent does first." We started playing and kind of just silently moved the pieces.

"Ahem." I tried to break the silence. "So... How come your name is spelled the same way as the word that means, you know, the organ in your head."

Brain looked up. "Well, it was kind of a mistake," he said. "My parents actually knew a guy name Brein that saved my dad's life. He was a foreign doctor over here for a work-study," he continued. I moved my pawn two spaces forward.

"What is wrong with your dad?" I asked. He instantly killed my pawn with a knight. *Ugh, dang it.*

"He had some sort of stroke and he fell into a coma." Brain said. "But Brein saved his life."

"Huh that's cool," I said.

"Yeah, you know what else is cool?"

"What?" I asked.

He smiled. "Checkmate." He knocked over my king with his finger. We started to laugh.

"Dang it," I said chuckling. "Well how did that turn into Brain?"

Brain started to set back up the pieces.

"Well to honor him for saving my dad's life, they were going to name me Brein, which is also pronounced Brian. On the paperwork the nurse dutifully wrote down Brein but the "e" looked like an "a" because it was smudged. When my parents got the official birth certificate, they spotted the error. After only a few weeks they had thought that I was such a smart kid that this was serendipity or something.

They just left the spelling that way and never fixed it. They still called me Brian though."

He continued, "When I got older and got made fun of, they would always tell me it made me 'unique.' Eventually, I learned not to listen to the teasing. But it does still come up and it is more annoying than anything."

We moved the pieces. "Wow, and I thought I had problems. Let's change the subject then. What team do you think is gonna win the competition?" I asked him.

He thought for a moment. "I think that it's gonna be a close game," he said while he moved his pawn.

"Me too." I knocked over his pawn with my bishop.

"You know my brother was on the Red Team," Brain said.

"He's here?" I asked a little surprised.

"No, no. He was here a couple years ago," he said.

"He said Red Team has better tents, but I think he's lying."

"Do you think it's weird how they let us play capture the flag with that awful weather?" I moved my queen to his side of the board.

"It is weird," Brain said. "I mean, someone could

have injured themselves. The lawyers would have had a field day, and this place would be closed down forever."

"It doesn't seem smart."

"You'll think I'm crazy for this, but you know when we were running from the giant tree? I could've sworn I saw someone watching us from the woods," Brain told me. I blinked.

"What like a Red Team camper?" I asked him.

"No, it was like a large man," he said. Brain killed my queen with his knight. "It was kind of creepy."

I thought for a moment about what he just said. "What if it was that Mikey?"

"I told you that was a myth," Brain said.

"What else would you explain a shadowy man in the woods with?"

He thought for a moment. "I don't know." I was never a huge fan of chess, but this seemed to be a pretty cool way to pass the time on a relaxing day.

After being hunched over that chess board for what seemed like hours I got up and went to stretch my legs. I walked to the outskirts of the camp site and headed down the main path. *I gotta say, at least it isn't really buggy at this camp.* It seemed to get dark pretty quickly—there was never enough lights on the camp paths and I didn't bring my flashlight.

I walked a bit faster along the gravel trail to head back to the campsite while I could still see. Luckily we were at the best campsite in the whole place. This site was close to everything. I walked by the sign that said Sleepy Hollow. This was starting to feel like a special place. *Oh no! Were my parent's right? Am I making special memories? Ugh, I cannot let them know they are right about this or anything. I'll never hear the end of it.*

"Hey, home hog, wanna play a game?" I looked over toward the little gazebo where Z was sitting with Jake.

"Sure," I said as I walked over.

"Some more cards?" I asked. As I got closer I could see in the dim light of Z's lantern that they were playing UNO.

"Yeah, but this game kind of sucks," Jake groaned.

"Fine, wez can play Presidents."

"What's that?" I asked Z.

"Cardz," he said casually.

"What? No the game," I said.

"Oh here I'll explain," Z said to me. He explained how to play the game called Presidents. It was a weird game where you put a card in the middle of the table and the bigger the number the better the card. The one with the biggest card won the hand. I went first and put a three of clubs in the middle of the table. Jake immediately put down a four.

"See you guyz got it," Z said. He put down a six of hearts.

"What do you guys think about the whole Red Team thing?" I asked everyone.

"I'm actually friends with some of the kids on Red Team," Jake said.

"Really?" Z asked.

"Yeah my friend Joey is on Red Team. He goes to the same school as me. We like to play basketball. That kid is really fast. Strong too." Jake put down a king. It was Z's turn to put down a card. He put down a two of clubs.

"Woah, wait, a two is way lower than a king!" I said.

"No in thiz game, the two be the highest cardz."

"What, that's dumb," Jake said.

"Hey to bez fair I didn't make thiz game." Z slid the cards to the dead pile where all the cards go when you can't play a higher card. Z put down two fours on the table.

"Thiz iz called doublez. Itz when you putz down

two cards then youz guyz have to put down two of the same card thaz be higher than these two," Z explained. I put down two fives, which were the only cards I could play.

"I don't have any," Jake said.

"Then you can just say pass."

"Pass," Jake said. Z put down another two of spades.

"Dude how come you have all the twos?" I asked.

"'Cause he's cheating, he dealt the cards!" Jake said.

"That would be against the card players code!" Z said.

"What the heck is the card players code?" Jake asked.

"When I went to this card game camp earlier this summer I had to take an oath called the card pla—"

"The card players code. Yeah, I get it," I said.

"Yo, I won!" Jake shouted. I looked over at Jake, who had gotten rid of all his cards so I guess that meant he won.

"Good job, broski," Z said to Jake. Z put down double eights.

I couldn't play it. "Pass."

Z scooted the cards to the end of the table. He

put down a five, which was his last card. "Citizen!" he shouted.

"What?" I said.

"Oh whoever wins is president, and I'm a citizen because I'm second and you dude, youz got scum."

"That's right you pile of swamp scum!" Jake yelled.

"Geez calm down," I said to Jake. Z shuffled and dealt the cards again.

"Okay, so since youz be scum, you have to give Jake, the president, two of your best cards and he will give you two cards of his choosing." Jake gave me two cards face-down and I gave him a king and a two.

"Give me something good," I said to Jake.

I looked at the cards. It was a three and a five. I looked up at Jake, who was chuckling to himself. We played Presidents until around 4 a.m. Z was asleep on the table drooling everywhere.

"C'mon let's go back to the tents," I said to Jake.

"Nah, I'm going to draw a handlebar on the card-player here."

"Dude remember what happened to me when I did that?" I told him.

"I don't care." He uncapped a sharpie and drew a big ol' mustache on Z. "Hey do you see that wrench in the shelf over there?" Jake said to me.

I looked over at a shelf on the wall covered in webs with a wrench on it. "Uh yeah, why do you need it?" I asked him.

"Just give it to me it's really important."

I reached my hand into the shelf. "Ugh it's so gross." I grabbed the wrench and put it down on the table.

"Thanks," Jake said and continued to draw on Z's face.

"Are you gonna use it?" I asked him.

"Huh? No," he said.

"Oh okay," I said. "Wait, what?"

Jake started to laugh hysterically. I grabbed the wrench and slid it across the table so it would fall onto his lap.

"Ew!" he screamed. He picked up the marker. "Come here!"

"No not again!" I shouted. I ran around the gazebo to tried and outrun him. We spent the rest of the night just goofing around. It was pretty nice to just have some fun.

THE RACE WITH NO ONE

I was trapped under the ice. I don't know how I got here, but I knew I only had seconds to spare. I would run out of air soon. I was pounding upward against the thick frozen sheets, determined to live. It was really cold when I woke up. My dreams here at camp were getting weirder. Trapped under ice? I shivered. It was very strange for a summer morning to be this chilly, but it always seemed cold in the morning here for some reason. I got out of bed to change into my clothes.

"Ugh, good morning, home hog," Z grumbled and rolled out of his cot.

"Good morning Z." I put on my shoes and opened the tent flaps. It was a little cloudy. I yawned and walked over to the little gazebo at the center of the campsite.

The Sleepy Hollow campsite was the best laid out of all the sites I saw. It had a ring of tents and an opening between where the gravel path to all the activities are held. In the middle of the dozen or so tents was a little gazebo with a couple benches under it. We usually sat there in the morning to wait for everyone to get out of bed.

"Hey there," Brain called out. He invited me to walk over.

"Do you know what they have for breakfast?" I asked Brain. I hoped it was something other than sausages and eggs again because it was starting to gross me out eating the same thing over and over again.

"Yeah I think they're having sausages and eggs," Brain said. I banged my head on the table as an exaggeration for my outrage, which I instantly regretted. "OW!"

Jake came over with Z strolling behind.

The rest of the kids in our campsite made their way over. Bill came out of his tent with a ton of energy, as usual.

"Alright guys, you ready to go to breakfast?" he

called to everybody. He waited as if he wanted someone to respond. "Okay, let's go then!"

We walked down the old gravel path, made of tiny rocks and pebbles. Up ahead I could see the beach. We took a right and saw the familiar big white tent where we ate almost every meal. *More like a grub tent than a dining hall.* We walked in and sat down at our table with the rest of camp.

"Uh, excuse me," some tall counselor dude with a short dark beard said.

"You have KP today," he told me.

"Okay," I replied, having no idea what that was.

"Uh, guys, what's KP?" I asked my friends.

"Oh, kitchen patrol. It's like when you just help out before and after a meal."

"So what, I just help cook eggs?" I asked them.

"Most likely you'll be sweeping up leftover eggs off the floor," Jake said.

"Eww." I made a face. Then I remembered the food fight and felt bad for whoever had KP that day. I didn't even know it was a thing back then.

"C'mon kid we got some spilled sausages!" the man with the beard said.

"Ha, see there are no eggs!" I got a mop and headed out to clean up the mess with the sausages.

"Hey, can you refill that jug of water over there?" the guy asked.

"Okay." I filled it up with one of those big gallon buckets of water. Then after breakfast I had to stay to help clean up the mess after. Luckily everyone was pretty clean, and I only had to sponge down the tables and that was pretty much it!

I started to walk out of the dining hall intending to leave, but the tall counselor with the beard stopped me. "I have a reward for you." He told me. In his hands was an envelope which he handed to me.

"What's this?" I asked.

"I handle all the mail for the camp in addition to doing KP. It looks like you got some." He said, then he walked away. I put the envelope in my back pocket and walked back to Sleepy Hollow.

When I got back to the campsite, I saw a lot of kids that looked ready to go somewhere. "Hey, Z, where are you guys going?" I asked him.

"Wez getting ready for the race!" Z replied.

"What race?" I asked. I hadn't thought I'd ever see a situation in which Z would *want* to race.

"Wez gonna race to thiz Magic Rock!" Z said.

I chuckled. "What does it do, grant wishes?"

"Thaz just be the name home hog. I don't know," Z said.

I guessed we were gonna race the Red Team to this big rock and whoever got there first would win the day's competition. I was still fuzzy about what we were supposed to be doing, but I figured everyone else had a plan. I would just go along for the ride.

"On your mark! Get set! Go!" Bill shouted suddenly. In a flash everyone started running down the trail.

"So where is Red Team?" I asked Z as we jogged down a little muddy path. *I don't think I've been this way before.* This was some sort of back route to somewhere. Hopefully to the rock.

"Theyz be racing on the other side, broski."

Slowly I started figuring out what the event was. The boulder rock thing had two paths that lead to it which were the same distance and we were gonna race down the two paths. Some kid up ahead of us jumped over a puddle and badly calculated the distance. He slipped straight into it. He sank surprisingly deep. "Help!" he shouted from inside the mud, his head and hand reaching out of it.

"Oh my god. Z, did you see that!?" I looked over at Z who was dripping with sweat and panting. It was rather impressive that a kid like Z could move when he wanted to. I was still thinking about the kid drowning in the mud. I looked back to see if he was still there. He was gone! I was going to turn back and help him up, but then I saw the finish line to our little race. The Magic Rock!

I didn't see what was so magic about it. It was covered in a bunch of graffiti and spray paint. Okay, it was almost twenty feet high, but still just a big rock.

"Woohoo! We won, home hog!" Z shouted. He was right; Red Team wasn't here, which did mean that we won.

I looked at the boulder and saw someone trying to scale it and recognized the black beanie. Huh, that's where Jake had been—out in front. I tried to climb onto the boulder and get to the top.

"Hey, Z, come on!" I invited him to climb on the rock as well.

"What's up Jake?" I nodded, and he grinned at me. I think he liked being the first up top. Once everyone got an eyeful of us they all hopped up onto the rock.

Oh there is the mud kid I thought. He was absolutely filthy, but at least he didn't drown.

"Hey Red Team still isn't here!" someone called out. I laughed but slowly I realized they were right. It had been like five minutes and we still hadn't seen the Red Team. Up the path came the skinny frame of Brain. He looked exhausted and kept holding his finger up in the air. I think he wanted to tell us something, but he was winded.

"Hey, Z, are you sure that this is Magic Rock?" I asked him in a slight panic. He pulled a little foldable map out of his back pocket and looked at it for a minute.

"Uhh, broski, I got some bad newz," Z said. "Wez went to the wrong rock."

"What?" I said.

Brain finally said from down below, "I've been trying to tell you guys. You went the wrong way!"

Everybody turned to Z. "Hey who's idea was it to come this way?" someone shouted. The group then turned to some kid in a baseball cap.

"Hey don't look at me!" he squealed.

"Get 'em!" someone shouted. The kid jumped off the rock and made a run for it. While everyone raced after that kid, Z, Jake, Brain, and I started walking back to our campsite. I was a bit disappointed, but then again, I didn't even really know what was going on today.

We didn't really have anything else planned, so Z and I split off so we could take a nap. I was tired anyway. All the time at camp was catching up to me, not to mention the exertion from the race with no one. Is it a race if you don't have an opponent?

"Ugh good night, home hog," Z said.

"Okay but it's not technically night though," I tried to tell Z but he was already snoring. *Meh okay.* I stretched out and relaxed on my cot.

Before I went to sleep I remembered that envelope I had gotten earlier. I pulled it out of my jeans back pocket. It was from my mom. I tried to open it neatly but failed, so I ripped it open.

Dear Julian,

I hope you are having fun at camp! I was thinking about you today and how you are becoming a handsome young man. I know camps like these can be trying on you. You might get lonely or homesick. Maybe the weather or activities aren't all that you want them to be. Perhaps some people are annoying you. These are all problems you will face in life. Your ability to work through these things (on your own) is what helps you develop character. That is never easy. I know that you have been taking care of yourself more now that it's just you and me, (and of course Remmy). That is the mark of someone growing into adulthood. It means you are becoming someone who can stand on their own. That, by the way, is the greatest accomplishment for any parent; to raise a child who can problem solve, overcome insecurity, and find a way to be successful.

Love,
    Mom

I stared at the paper, almost tearing up but I wiped my eyes before the waterworks could come. I flipped the paper over and picked up a pencil from my backpack so I could write a letter to her as well.

Dear Mom,
    It's nice to hear from you. I am having a good time and making lots of friends. It has been really cold here and I can't wait to get back into a real bed again. Say hi to Remmy for me.

Love,
    Julian

I DECIDED I would give the letter to the mail dude tomorrow. I put the letter in my backpack, then I closed my eyes, thinking about the letter and what my Mom wrote me.

I must have fallen asleep because I woke up to the sounds of people shouting random words like "pterodactyl!" And "chicken on fire!" I opened up my tent flaps to see that people were playing charades outside. I ignored it. It was sunset, so I went to the bathroom and decided to just go back to sleep. I hadn't gotten this much sleep in a long time.

I woke up one more time that night to get a jacket. The nights here got really cold so I found a hoodie to put on and went into my bed again. I was a little bummed out by the Magic Rock thing because that means that the Red Team technically won another competition. *I'm sure that Rick and his team are celebrating.* I was getting worried about the competition. It seemed like Red always had the upper hand.

I wonder what my mom would think if I came home with a big shiny trophy. Then she could see that there was no need to worry about me. Oh no! I hadn't realized that me and Z had slept through dinner. I was definitely hungry. I looked over at Z's bed. I saw that he had several wrappers along the side of his bed. I saw an untouched Quaker bar that I could grab. Not the best dinner I'd had here but I'd take what I could get. Then it was back to sleep.

I f you wake up hours before the sun comes up, is that technically still night? It was dark out and I couldn't see anything. I was thankful for the glow function on my watch, which told me it was 4 a.m. It was actually warm, which was surprising. I walked out of my tent and noticed there was something out in front. I squinted to try and see what on earth it was. It was tall and bendy and had weird hair. The hair looked like fingers—they *were* fingers. It was a hand! It jumped up and grabbed me by the neck and pinned me down! "Help!" The hand pinned me down even harder.

"Wake up!" it screamed.

"Wakez up, home hog!" it screamed louder. I

jumped up with a start and saw that I was in my cot, and Z was staring at me in his pajamas.

I must have been shaking or something in my sleep because he looked worried. "Oh uh," I responded, trying to shrug off my weird dream to Z but he didn't buy it.

"What time is it?" I asked him. He pulled out his phone and pressed the power button.

"Uh, letz see. About 5:45ish, broski," he said. I plopped my head back on the pillow. I knew I had about an hour until I had to get up for breakfast. I looked up and saw my *Starry Night* painting. It looked the same as usual with its bright pink paint splatters. I looked over near Z's cot and saw his burger painting, but it had scratches on it. It didn't look like an animal did it. There were just slit holes in it, almost like a knife had passed through it. *Mikey?*

Hey Zack, uh, do you know why your painting has holes in it?" I asked.

He looked up from his cot and shrugged. "I don't know maybez some animalz of somez sorts."

"But the holes—" I started.

"Ugh, let me go to sleep," he said. *What on earth would do that?* I stared at the roof of the tent for what seemed like an eternity when someone bolted into our tent.

"AH!" I screamed and threw my lantern at the intruder. The glass shattered over the person's head.

"Ack!" They sputtered and fell to the ground. I saw who I hit. It was Jake coming in to wake up me and Z. I got out of my cot quickly.

"Oh my gosh! Are you okay Jake!" I asked as he slowly tilted his head up.

"Do me a favor," he said. "You see that truck out there." I looked out of my plastic window and saw a truck out in the middle of our campsite.

"Go under it. I'll get behind the wheel. I'm gonna run you over," he said as he was rubbing his head. Z from the other side of the room burst out laughing. Jake got up and dusted pieced of glass off him. He saw *Starry Night* on my wall.

"Nice painting," he said.

"C'mon, Dumb and Dumber. Time for Breakfast," Jake said. We walked out of our tents to go to the dining hall. As we walked down the trail I tripped on a rough root.

"Hey watch where you're going," Jake barked.

I pushed my hands out to get up but then I noticed something near the root I'd tripped on. By the tree there was a little sticky note. I picked it up. It read *Twired Coyote Showcase: Team Leader B. Decided to stay at Lumberjack Woods*. I stared at the page for a moment. "Yo, home hog, lez get outta here. We got stuff to do!" Z shouted back at me from a couple yards away. I hurried over with the rest of them. They had eggs and sausages as usual. We sat down at our table after we grabbed our food.

"Geez, these sausages seem kind of gross," I said looking down at my plate.

"Yeah because they're probably made of crow," Brain said.

"Crow?" Jake asked.

"It's a thing from a TV show I like."

"Nobody cares," I said sarcastically.

"Geez, man, calmz yourself. Go easy on the guy huh?"

"Ugh the pain. I'm gonna barf," Jake said bluntly. I poked my eggs with my fork. *They look like rubber*. Not the best day as far as breakfast went.

I tried to figure out what the note I found meant. I told my buddies about what was written on it. "What the heck does twired mean?" Jake asked me.

"It means watch or to peek out of," Brain butted in. "But that's old English."

"So there's a bunch of coyotes spying on the Blue Team for their showcase?" Jake asked sarcastically.

"It's probably an anagram for something," Brain told us.

I sipped my orange juice. "What does it mean then?"

"I'm not sure. I've never been good with anagrams."

"Thaz if it iz an anagram cracker," Z said with his mouth full of sausages.

It could be something to do with Mikey. I took a bite into my sausage. "What do you guys think about that Mikey thing?"

"Hoax," Brain said.

"Dude that's the stupidest thing in the world," Jake said, eyeing the salt at the edge of the table.

"Can you pass the salt?" he asked.

"I thinkz that Mikey story could be real. Ya know, dudez?"

"But no one's ever seen him!" Brain protested.

"Guys, the salt?" Jake said.

"Maybe he captures people when they see him so no one will ever know!"

"That's absurd!" Jake tried to get the salt but couldn't reach.

"How do youz know hez not real!?"

"There's no such thing as a guy who has lived in a shack with no food for years on end!"

"Maybe he eats berries!"

"Berries!?" Jake was lying on the table trying to get the salt.

"He's real!" Z grabbed the salt and put some on his eggs.

Jake got angry. "Give me the salt!"

"Calmz yourself, home hog!" Z screamed. I tried to break up the fight.

"He was probably made up by some goof ball trying to scare kids!" Brain told Z.

"Give me the salt!" Jake screamed and tried to punch Z in his chubby face.

"Hey what are you kids doing! Sit down!" A camp counselor said. I slumped down in the bench trying not to be associated with the incident.

"The orange juice!" someone in the distanced screamed.

"Hey!" the counselor said and ran off to the mess on the floor. A barrel of orange juice spilled out all over the floor. We all looked at each other.

"This camp is crazy," I said.

"Agreed," they all said in unison. We realized that it was about time to clean up our food. We scrubbed down our table with a sponge and threw our leftovers in the trash, which was a lot because the food was awful. We looked at the clock.

"Hey, home hog, shouldn't we be going to the—"

"Next challenge? Yeah you're right let's go," Jake said as he got up and started walking out of the dining hall. There were a bunch of people crowding outside the dining hall. I went closer to see what all the commotion was about. There was a huge truck that had multiple boxes in the back of it. It was a large silver beast with huge wheels and a lot of smoke coming out of the exhaust pipe.

I saw that Rick and Bill, the Team Red and Team Blue counselors come out of the two doors. "No, I'll do it!" Rick whispered to Bill.

"Attention, campers!" Rick shouted out.

"Today, we will be having a survival shelter-building contest." Everyone looked at each other. I knew what this was. Bill had told me about the survival shelter building and gave me a link in a flash drive. I was ready for this challenge.

"Alright everyone. Red Team will come with me and Blue Team can go with Bill," said Rick.

Bill walked over to me. "You watched the video I gave you, right?" he asked me.

"Yeah, I'm ready," I said trying to act confident.

He smiled and patted me on the shoulder and said, "Now let's go win this thing, okay?"

We walked over with the rest of Blue Team.

Everyone was chattering about how hard this was going to be, but I knew I could help lead us to victory. I stepped up on the side of the silver truck so I was above the crowd.

"Uh, hello!" I shouted, "Uh, well this may seem hard, but I know we can do it." Was that me? Where did that come from? Bill was nodding at me. Some people looked at me sarcastically like I had no idea what I was doing.

"I know how to build a shelter," I continued. "I can even build one good enough to sleep in, in under ten minutes." That's about when people started to look up like they actually had some hope in this competition.

"Alright, guys. You can do this," Bill responded. Some people were nodding their heads now.

"Let's do this!" someone from the crowd shouted. Then Z and Jake were cheering and then Brain. Everyone was getting excited.

"The place where we will be setting up camp is called Lumberjack Woods," said Blue Leader Bill. That name sounded familiar. *The note.* He started to follow a dirt path that probably led to the place he was talking about. Everyone got in a line behind him. We followed him for about three minutes when we suspected he was not taking us to the challenge area.

At least not directly. I had a better plan – I stopped in to the Trading Post gift shop as we walked by to get a map. That will help me find Lumberjack Woods.

"Hey there, snoozer," the shopkeeper said as he greeted me.

"Hey there. Do you have a map that shows how to get to Lumberjack Woods?"

"Ya see that corner o'er there? There are some maps over there next to the soda machine," he said back to me. I saw the rack of maps for Camp Golden Hills.

"Thanks, sir." I grabbed a map, paid for it and headed out on my way to the forest. It was a long walk with a couple of wrong turns but I made it to Lumberjack Woods on time. I say on time – there were already kids here who were in line with Bill, so maybe they did come straight here? I should trust my gut less I think.

I saw an open plain in the middle of the woods where we would set up camp. There was a pile of boxes in the middle of the area. I walked over to go see what they were and I opened one up and saw lots of rope.

"It's for tying down the sticks," said Brain as he walked by with a box. I knew that though because I had already practiced. I looked around for some good trees that had a lot of dead branches so I could make a nice shelter. I found a tall tree that I thought was completely dead. It had no leaves and looked really pale. *Perfect. Just what I need.*

I snapped off tons of branches. There were no more left on the tree when I was done. I figured I'd use the tree as part of my shelter too. I leaned some sticks against the side of the tree and made a cozy little room with some sticks. I went around to some more trees and got some leaves and covered the sticks in them to have and extra layer. I saw a maple tree with oozing maple sap coming out of it. I went over and filled my empty box of rope with some of the sap. Then I dipped the leaves into the sap and made an even better shelter than I had at home because now the leaves were sticky and wouldn't blow off of the sticks at night.

I had spent nearly forty minutes building my shelter, despite having made a shelter in ten minutes at home. But this time, I made the shelter bigger! I looked over and saw Z. He was really struggling. I had to help him. His shelter was falling apart. I told him about the maple sap thing and he saw the tree and ran over to it. I think all of Blue Team's shelters looked pretty nice. In fact Jake and Brain decided to combine their shelters, so they had a super huge one. Z's looked like a hobbit hole, but still kind of roomy. He had actually built a window with a plastic water bottle he'd cut out so it would unfold into a clear flat window. Everyone else's looked good too. Someone had tried to make theirs look like a castle. One looked like a military base. One shelter even looked like it was a UFO or something. Mine was supposed to look like a cottage. I was going for something small and cozy.

The ultimate goal was to be able to spend the night in our shelters. After lunch, we were able to get out camping gear. From the Sleepy Hollow campsite I got my lantern, blanket, and pillow. My shelter was small, but I was able to stuff all my gear in it. As I was doing so, I noticed a big rock about the size of my door. I was able to put it in front of the door and used it as an actual door.

I heard a knock on the rock. Z moved the rock out of the way and handed me a water bottle and some scissors.

"What's this for?" I asked.

"Windowz broski," he told me.

I chugged the water bottle and cut it up so I could use it as a crinkly window. I clicked on my lantern and set it to the lowest setting for a while.

Before I went to sleep, I clicked it off. Even though I put layers onto my shelter and had a blanket, I was still freezing. There were holes in the sides of my window Z gave me. Maybe I shouldn't have used it.

I couldn't sleep, so I turned on my light. It got dark faster than I thought up here at Lumberjack Woods. The trees were blocking the moonlight. I looked out my little plastic bottle window and saw Z jiggling around, trying to get comfy in his cramped confined space. I saw Bill was sleeping in the silver truck. Why was he so eager to help me? I felt like he had more of a story to tell. I guess I could ask him what his story was tomorrow, but I felt kind of awkward asking him. *Did he go to this camp when he was my age? Did he feel sorry for me? Is that why he helped me?* I felt a little annoyed. I didn't want him to feel sorry for me. *I'm fine on my own, I can take care of my own stuff.*

Something caught my eye. There was something caught on a nearby pine tree. It looked like... *paper?* I squinted to see what it was, what it said, but I knew what it was. It was the poster from my first night at camp. It said, "die, you."

I didn't sleep at all. It was too cold and my body just couldn't handle it. I was afraid if I fell asleep I would freeze to death. By morning and when it was time to get up, I had huge bags under my eyes. You could even say I had luggage under my eyes the bags were so big. I had to use all of my strength to push the big rock out of the way to get out of my shelter. I looked over at Z's shelter and saw that he had fallen asleep soundly. I was ready to just fall asleep standing up right there and fall down on the floor.

Bill was also having a nice sleep when he slipped and smacked his face into the truck's horn. BWAH! It blared until Bill noticed what he was doing. I was fine with it because the horn more or less woke me up. Then everyone got out of their shelters. We all gathered around the truck and waited for Bill to announce the next horrible task for the day. I guessed today's task was gonna be awful.

"Ahem! Well, campers. Uh, today you can do whatever you want!" Bill announced. I had guessed wrong.

"What?" Brain asked.

"Well the only thing for today was to see whose shelter was the best so, uh, just don't ruin your shelter and we'll win the competition... probably," said Bill.

"What do you mean probably?" I asked.

"Well it depends how good Rick's shelters are," he told me. I looked around at all the shelters. Some were certainly better than others.

Bill came over to me. "Hey, I can tell you're worried."

"How do you know?" I said.

"I was just like you when I was your age. I went to this camp so many years ago and when I was here, I wasn't the leader I should have been. Like you are."

"Me? A leader?" I chuckled.

"When I was here as a camper, we also had a shelter-building contest. It was worse than you have it now. If you lost, you would spend the last night sleeping in the other team's shelters and they would always destroy them before you arrived, so you would just end up sleeping out in the open air," Bill said.

"When my team lost, I weaseled out and tried to run away. At the time, the camp directors got to sleep in separate cabins. They had just got new ones and I found one of the older abandoned ones," Bill continued. I waited for him to get to the point.

"When I went inside and saw lots of writing on the wall about some kid... uh, I forget the name... it was Mickey, or Michael, or something."

"Mikey.?" I said.

"Yeah! That was his name," he said and continued, "Gosh that legend scared me half to death. My brother Rick would torment me with scary stories all the time."

"You guys are brothers?" I asked as I smiled nervously.

"Yup. Anyway, I spent the night in that old shack and it was full of amazing things. For a camp, I mean. Things like a shower and a toilet with two-ply toilet paper. But the haunting thing about it was the fact that I was spending the night in an amazing place while I left everyone else to freeze," he said looking down at the ground.

"So, what do you want me to do?" I asked.

"I want you to stick with your team and if you haven't looked at the other camper's forts, maybe help them out today instead of hanging out and buying stuff from the Trading Post. Okay?" He looked me square in the eye and held out his hand. I outstretched mine and we shook on it.

Bill walked away onto the gravel path that led to the dining hall. It was mandatory to go to breakfast so I gathered up my tired strength and fought off my exhaustion. I trudged slowly over to the big white tent which kept flashing black because I was blinking really heavily. I eventually got there and had a quick bowl of cereal. I also noticed a coffee machine in the back of the tent! *When did this get here?* I thought to myself. I grabbed a mug and filled it up with some nice hot and steamy joe. I gulped it down in about three seconds. Time for the walk back to Lumberjack Woods. *I can't believe Rick and Bill are related. They seem so different. Wait until I tell the guys about that.*

I wandered around inspecting all the shelters everyone made. This was what they'd come up with? We were surrounded by a group of dead trees. *Hmm if this is Lumberjack Woods then there should be an axe around here somewhere.* I started searching through the forest until I found an axe laying against a tree. It didn't even looked that old. It was odd, but I didn't need to question that now.

I grabbed the axe and walked over to the large clearing where the shelters were located. Here were trees that looked as dead as a doornail and were perfect for building. With lots of branches of differing sizes and no leaves, this was the building material we needed. I took to it with the axe: HIK, HIK, HIK! I kept hacking away at the base of the first tree until it gave way and fell to its left side. The wood cracked loudly as it met its demise. It fell onto the ground hard with some of the branches cracking as they smacked into the ground.

I wiped some sweat from my brow and took some deep breaths. *Ugh, a lot of work to cut down a single tree.* Now there was a lot of wood to work with and there were a couple more dead trees if I needed more materials. I took the axe and chopped up the long thick log into pieces and threw them into a pile. I must say I was impressed with myself. I had cut down plenty of branches and there would be plenty of wood to help the other kids with their shelters.

By two p.m. I was ready to do some serious building. I started with Z's shelter and helped him make it about five times bigger. Now it had huge walls and even had a bed! I kept his plastic bottle window and built a window frame for it too. Now his shelter looked more like a fortress from a video game.

I decided to break for a late lunch, but instead of going to the dining hall, I just grabbed a meatball sub from the Trading Post. I passed on the gummy worms. I sat down on a stump in the middle of the open plain. I could see the sun was no longer in the middle of the sky but had begun its descent toward the horizon. *Better get moving.*

I got up and stuffed the leftover wrapping from my sandwich in my pocket and went over to my pile of wood. *Time to do some work on Jake and Brain's shelter.* They had worked on their shelter together and were happy to have the help. They had two rooms in there. Jake's "room" looked like a mess. I could see his black beanie in a pile of sticks that looked like camp hadn't treated it so well. I also saw that Jake had a Northface compass on the ground.

Brain's room was much neater, and he actually had walls that looked like walls. I decided to leave Brain's side as it was because it was pretty much perfect. Jake's was such a mess that I convinced him to just tear it down and start fresh. We tore it down and tried to make a copy of what Brain had built. I then gave him a roof. The roof was a branch from an evergreen tree with multiple pine needles on it. It would hopefully keep out the cold.

Around six p.m. it was time for dinner and I decided to call it a day. Tiredly, I walked back onto the path that lead back to the dining hall. I saw the bright lights that were only on at dinner and saw that almost all the tables were full. Almost because the one table that was always open was the peanut-free table, which no one sat at because nobody was allergic to peanuts. I sat down at the peanut-free table and waited until the counselors announced it was time to get food. I rapped my fingers on the tables and waited. *I know we're gonna win the shelter-building contest.* I kind of wanted to take a peek at the Red Team's shelters. You know, just to make sure we were gonna win the competition.

"Okay time to get yer dinner!" the lady called out from behind the metal trays of food. As I moved along the line, the lady asked me if I wanted some salad.

"What kind?"

"Caesar," she said in a high-pitched voice as she scrunched up her face.

Nobody was taking any salad and I kind of felt bad, so I said, "Sure."

During the commotion of people getting up for

food, I decided to sneak off into the Red Team's campsite. I think I knew where it was. It was somewhere north of Lumberjack Woods. I decided to grab Jake's compass from his shelter and use that to get me there. I picked it up and dutifully followed it north. The needle kept shaking back and forth and I kept taking crazy turns every dozen or so steps. Then it hit me, the compass was broken! I started to panic because now I was alone, in the dark, and lost.

I had to do something. I was wracking my brain —I had nothing. I pulled my arm out of my sweatshirt pocket and looked at my watch, 6:46 p.m. I panicked more because people were going to start wondering where I was. I looked for a light that would lead me back to anything. The Trading Post, the dining hall, a lantern, a campfire—anything. I finally saw a glimmer of light in the distance that looked like it may have been coming from a fire. As I walked closer, I saw that it was a fire. A slight sense of relief started to spread. I saw an old shack with a wooden sign that read "Twired Coyote Showcase." The sign was worn and didn't really stand out—but I was drawn to it anyway. That was the same thing on that note, and I hoped my theory on that note wasn't correct.

I never really bought any of this "Mikey" business. I was smarter than that, right? But I thought my heart was going to stop working from fear. I knew I had no other choice but to go inside. If I was here, the place that Bill had described, then I was nowhere near Lumberjack Woods. I opened the door and stepped inside. What I saw made my blood go cold. I wished I hadn't gone inside. Written on the wall, in deep red, were the words "Prepare to Die."

HOME ALONE

I stood there in the doorway and stared at the writing on the wall.

Why...Why... WHY IS THIS HERE?

My heart was beating so fast it felt like it was breaking my ribs. I thought I was gonna die from fear. I slapped myself in the face and tried to get ahold of myself. I took some deep breaths, but, inhaling, I noticed something odd. It smelled like paint in here. I walked inside the shack to see if anyone was actually here, and if there was any real danger other than my imagination. I heard the door behind me creak and then slam shut.

I turned around to see who did it. *The door just shut behind me. No big deal, that happens all the time,* I thought nervously. Did I hear footsteps coming toward me? No one was coming, at least that I could see.

I turned to run in the opposite direction of the noise and tripped over some cans of paint. I fell to the floor hard my hands taking most of the impact. Knocking over the cans made some loud clanging that scared me half to death. I was getting pretty jumpy. From here I could see a staircase further down the hallway. Springing to my feet, I looked down at the two paint cans I'd tripped over. I suddenly remembered my movie marathon of *Home Alone*. Grabbing the two paint cans, I ran toward the stairs. I still heard the click and clack of shoes behind me, but again, no one was there. Sweating bullets, I made it to the stairs. I could feel the energy draining from me and was too tired to walk any further—until I heard a scratchy voice say, "Who's there!"

My heart skipped a beat or two. I flew up the stairs faster than a cheetah with both paint cans in hand. Climbing up the stairs, I caught a glimpse of a man that looked like he was really angry. I screamed like a little girl and dropped the paint cans on top of him.

"AAH!" he screamed as the paint cans clanged on top of him. After the impact, he fell to the floor.

Did I just hit Mikey! Oh my god. Is he real?

I went higher up the stairs and came into an attic. It was full of rusty tools, a desk, and various types of camera equipment. I stepped inside and a siren started to blare the moment I walked into the room.

A robotic voice was saying something but it was distorted. Iinrdr lrt..." It looked like it was broken, simply hanging from the ceiling by a wire. I heard loud noises that sounded like more alarms outside the shack. I knew help was coming. I slammed the door to the attic shut before Mikey could get to me. I looked over to my right and saw a bunch of photos of Blue Team and us working on our shelters and an image of a canoe. I squinted to see the photo because it kind of looked like the canoe I had sank last week.

What does this mean?

The banging on the door got my pulse racing again. I took a chest full of gardening tools and put them in front of the door as a barricade.

"You're not supposed to be in here boy!" Mikey yelled from outside of the door.

I wish my dad was here to protect me! I fought back tears. I knew what was coming for me. I shut my eyes and got ready for the end. Then all the banging stopped, and all that was left were the sirens.

Why did he stop? Did he give up? I moved the chest from in front of the door and took a peek outside into the hallway. Nothing was there. I gave a sigh of relief and stepped out a little to try and run away. Then I saw someone in a black and yellow suit with what looked like a scary gas mask running down the hall toward me. This looked like it would be the last thing I saw before I got hit with the axe he was holding!

I screamed and slammed the door. *I can't do this! I can't do this! I'm not a leader! I'm gonna die! Please let me live!*

I gripped onto the edge of the chest, bracing it in front of the door. My legs were shaking, I could barely stand. His axe came smashing through the door. Wood chips were flying into my face. I let go of the chest and ran backward, almost falling down. I looked for a weapon so I could try and fight off Mikey before he could get through the door. I saw there was a lawnmower in the pile of tools in the room. I got behind it and pulled the rope hard to start it. RMMMM! RMMMM! It sputtered to life.

I think the throttle was stuck as it went flying from my grasp and straight toward the door. Before it got there, Mikey broke through the door with the axe.

He took one look at the mower coming toward him and chopped it down with his weapon.

Woah! He just destroyed a whole fricken lawn-mower! I was kind of impressed and terrified at the same time. I looked for anything I could use to defend myself and my eyes caught sight of a weed-whacker.

"I'm not letting you kill me Mikey!" I yelled as I turned it on.

"What? Kill you? What do you—" Mikey screamed from behind the mask. I squeezed my eyes closed and ran right at him with the weedwhacker roaring. *It was now or never.* He jumped the other way before I could hit him—I mean, I guess I should have kept my eyes open. The weedwhacker came into the wall and shredded the decaying wood. Then the motor conked out.

He saw his chance now that my weapon was out of the picture. He came over to me with his hands outstretched like he was going to grab me. I grabbed what was left of the weedwhacker and tried to throw it at him. It was too heavy, and I was exhausted. It just fell a couple feet in front of him. *This is it.* I closed my eyes and braced for death, but instead I got yelled at. "Kid, stop! What are you doing?!"

I looked at him closer and he reached up and

tugged some metal beads hanging down from the ceiling. A light switch. Now that the red light flickering wasn't the only light source, I could see him better now. I'd actually been fighting with a fireman. I put my palm to my forehead and gasped. *Oh no, I just tried to kill a fireman... and he was trying to rescue me. I'm a criminal!*

"Kid, what was that about? I'm here to rescue you. You've been missing," he told me through the mask. I looked over at the broken doorway which I had shut to keep the fireman from saving me. The man I had hit with the paint buckets walked into the room and typed some letters into a keypad near the door. The red lights and sirens stopped, and I saw who I had hit with the buckets. It was actually Rick, the Red Team counselor. *Oh no.* The sirens had actually been from the cops, I assumed. Although why would they come after me now when I went missing for a little bit? It didn't seem as odd as the other crazy things that went on at this camp.

"What was all the writing on the wall then?" I asked Rick.

"I wrote that here years ago as a joke for my brother." It just now dawned on me what Bill had said earlier about the prank with his brother and the shack. I looked around and realized what a disaster I had caused. I was probably gonna get kicked out of camp.

"Kid, come with me," Rick said in a low voice. I got up from the pile of wood I was sitting in and followed Rick into the hallway. I looked back at the fireman. He wouldn't take off his mask but he seemed familiar.

Rick lead me outside of the shack where a golf cart with the initials W.W. on it was parked. I looked around at the golf cart that was out here. I thought it was strange that a fireman came in a golf cart but it was the woods so maybe they were just easier to get around than a big truck. "What's the golf cart for?" I asked.

"To get you out of here," he told me, "Now get in." We got into the cart and he put the keys in the engine.

"Why didn't Bill come looking for me?" I asked him.

"He did. All the camp counselors did because it's just practical when searching," he said very quickly, but he didn't seem like he was telling the truth. We drove for about another five minutes until he brought me to the entrance to Lumberjack Woods.

"Why won't you go in?" I asked.

"I can't."

"Oh right," I replied. I remembered that there was still a competition between Red and Blue. He couldn't come in, so he wouldn't see the other shelters that we had built.

I stepped out of the golf cart and walked down the trail. I could hear him driving away in the background. Everyone in the campsite was already asleep. At least they were all just in their shelters. I looked into Z's plastic water bottle window and saw him snoring away. There were voices coming from Brain and Jake's shelter.

I walked over to my shelter, which still looked pretty amazing. I scraped the big rock door out of the way. It tore up the grass quite a bit, but it didn't really matter. *It'll grow back, won't it?* Settling inside, I got under my blanket. Technically it was a sleeping bag that was unzipped all the way. I rubbed my tired eyes yet again. It had been a long day. I yawned. I knew it was time to go to sleep. I looked up through my makeshift shelter roof at the crescent moon and gave a sigh of relief. I wasn't sure why, but I knew that we would win the competition tomorrow. I turned around and clicked the off button on my lantern, then I closed my eyes and went to sleep.

I bit into my pancake.

"I don't get it, why would they have pictures of Blue Team?" Brain asked, scratching his head.

"Iz be thinkin youz been thinkin too much about this whole spy coyote thing," Z told us.

"Twired Coyote Showcase," Brain corrected him.

"Whatevz," he said and sipped his orange juice.

I thought for a moment. "I'm going back to the shack today," I said.

"Good song," Jake said.

"What?" I asked.

"Back to the shack!" he said it like he was surprised we didn't know. He spread his T-shirt so it was easier to read. *Weezer.* it read. "It's a song, guys! You all have no taste in music." He slouched down.

"Ahem." Brain cleared his throat. "I think it would be a mistake for you to go back, you could get caught."

I just need to know what's going on there." I finished my breakfast quickly. "We're not doing anything today anyway. The counselors are deciding which team won.

"I'm coming too," Jake told me.

"Why?" I asked him. "You should stop asking me 'why' and just agree with me."

"I'm friends with—" He cut himself off. "I, uh, used to be friends with the kids on Red Team, I might know some useful stuff."

"Pass," Z said.

"I'm out too," Brain said.

"But you're the smart one!" I told him.

"Truly I'm flattered but I don't want to get in trouble." We kept on pressing him to join us until he agreed. "Fine," he finally said, and we headed out of the big white tent or and walked over to where I thought the shack was. Z watched us walk about 20 steps and then caved and caught up to us.

For a while we just walked through the woods in silence. I remembered what I was thinking last night. How I had thought I wasn't really good enough to be a leader? I had wished my dad was around to protect me. That made me a little upset. I didn't like how he had moved out of the house. I was always angry at my mom for that; she thought he was too lazy and couldn't hold a steady job. I always thought of him as the fun guy who would play catch with me outside and help me with my baseball practice.

But every time I thought of my mom as a villain, I saw how much stress she had on her shoulders. So, I had to back up and just let her think everything was fine; she didn't need to worry about me too. I always told her I could take care of myself, and I didn't need any help. When my dad left I tried to become the man of the house, but then that just stressed me out. It made me feel kind of weak.

I tried to cheer myself up. *Well I was strong enough to fight off that firefighter guy last night.* But that only made me feel like some sort of criminal who had tried to attack someone who was trying to help me. I looked up at Jake. I could tell he had something more underneath that tough outer layer. He wasn't a criminal, but I could tell he knew things that a kid his age shouldn't know.

"What do you mean you used to be friends with

the Red Team kids? Are you like, a spy?" I asked him carefully.

"No dude, they're just mad at me." We stepped over a log. "They were put on Red and I got put on Blue. So, they asked me to switch and I said no."

"They were mad at you for that?" Brain asked.

"They're not the best kids," he said, but I felt like that wasn't the whole story.

"Wait, where even is this 'shack' of yours," he asked, annoyed.

I got nervous. "Uh, I... don't know exactly," I said through my teeth.

"Nice," he grunted. Jake looked around at the trees and leaves on the ground.

"What are you doing?" Brain asked.

He stopped turning his head when he saw a large pine tree. "Perfect." Then he started climbing it much faster than I could have done. Pine trees are not the easiest to climb. There is sap on the branches and there are so many of them poking out everywhere. You have to weave your way through them only stepping on the ones thick enough to hold you while avoiding the rest. I had to admire that feat - it took some skill.

"Wow!" Brain shouted. Clearly he was impressed too.

"Yeah," he said with a smirk. "It's over there." He pointed.

"How close is it?" I asked.

"Not far. Can't be more than a couple football fields away." He jumped down from the tree and then we continued our search.

A few minutes later the building came into view. "That's it!" I yelled excitedly.

Jake rolled his eyes. "Chill, man." He walked over towards the shack and I followed.

I approached the door and reached for the door-knob, but Jake slapped my hand.

"Ow! What are you—" He cut me off.

"Don't use the door, you fool!" he said quietly with a finger over his mouth to shush me. He looked up and around taking in all the things that he could potentially use. "Grab that ladder over there so I can look at the window. We don't want to be seen or heard. I need to make sure the coast is clear."

I grabbed this wooden, old ladder that was leaning on the side of the shack. It had the initials W.W. carved on it. "What does W.W. even mean?" I asked. He grabbed the ladder out of my hands and put it down.

"Hopefully we're about to find out," Brain said in

a hushed voice. Jake climbed up and pulled down his beanie so it covered his face.

"Can you see?" I asked him.

"Yeah it's a thin hat. When it's stretched it is practically see through. I can see out but people or cameras can't see my face." He looked through the window. It kind of troubled me how much Jake knew about how to check out a place without being seen. These aren't typical teenager skills I thought, but it was useful anyhow.

"The coast is clear." He lifted up his beanie so it was at the top of his head again. With a little bit of muscle he was able to open the window and he promptly climbed in.

"Could've just used the door if the coast was clear." I mumbled as I climbed up the ladder and pulled myself through the window. We started to take in the room as our eyes adjusted.

Brain was the next through the window. "Where's Z?" I whispered.

"He is going to stay on lookout duty." Brain stated, "But I think he is acrophobic."

"What?" I gestured to him with my shoulders shrugging.

"Fear of heights." Brain said - clearly exasperated with me.

"Oh, my lord!" Jake exclaimed. He furrowed his brow and scowled at me.

Now what? My wreckage was still there for all to see. "Oh uh..." I shuffled my feet sheepishly.

"You left so much evidence." Again, his response was concerning.

I averted my eyes and started looking around the shack again. There were some video cameras lying on the floor, and some old tools for gardening. As I crossed the room I stepped over a shovel. There was a sturdy looking desk in the corner of the room, which I'd seen a glimpse of the night before. Above the beaten up desk were the images I had seen on my last visit here.

"There's the pictures I was talking about!" I pointed. I leaned in closer and looked at the pictures posted on the wall. The picture of the canoe up there was definitely mine.

"Did they purposely sink the boat I was using?" I asked. "How did they know I would take that one?"

"Maybe they weren't targeting you but just anyone on the Blue Team." Jake gasped. "Then everyone would have had to stop racing and try to see what happened!"

"A possibility, but the teams weren't a thing yet," Brain reminded him.

He thought about that for a moment. "You're right." He looked again at the pictures of the campers.

"What's in the desk?" Brain asked. I pulled open a drawer. It had a bunch of binders and notebooks, various papers scattered, some odds & ends. Like most desk drawers.

"Oh nice, there's homework in the desk," Jake remarked.

I started to flip through some of the notebooks. Nothing in this one. The next not much of anything either. Then I saw something that caught my eye. "Guys! Come check this out," I said.

Brain leaned over behind me. "The Mikey mystery has been an excellent cover for W.W," Brain read aloud.

"I still cannot believe the prank is still going," I finished.

Jake came over. "What prank?"

"Is W.W. some joke group?" Brain asked.

I looked at the images on the wall. "No that can't be it, some of these incidents were pretty serious." I said.

I read over the words on the paper again. I opened the side drawer and pulled out one of the binders. It was a thick one - maybe three inches and held a lot of stuff. I opened it up and looked inside. "It seems to be just just a bunch of bills," I said.

"Invoices you mean. Like for camera equipment." Brain told me. "These cameras appear to be bought under the camp's name." Brain pointed to Camp Golden Hills written on the name slip.

I cocked my eyebrow. "Why would the camp fund spy equipment?" I wondered.

Jake was pressing his ear on the door and quickly motioned to us all. "Guys we got to get outta here!" No sooner than he said that, we heard footsteps coming towards the door. I quickly grabbed the notebook and the huge binder, but I fumbled around and dropped the binder on the ground. SLAM! It hit the ground hard. Jake was already climbing back out the window with Brain practically on top of him. He stopped for a second and stared at me.

"Who's in there?" someone yelled on the other side of the door. It wasn't Rick though, the voice sounded younger... and familiar. The door handle was starting to turn. I quickly jumped out the window. In my hurry I missed a step. CRASH! I landed in some leaves and mud which kind of broke the fall. Before I could react, Jake jumped out onto his feet and pushed over the ladder.

"Run!" he whisper-screamed at me. Z and Brain

were nowhere to be seen. I sprinted away and once I was in the tree line I dared to look back. I saw a familiar face looking out the window, it was the pink sling kid. Gerald.

"Why would he be in the shack?" Jake asked.

I put down my fork. "I have no idea. Maybe he got lost too?"

"He asked 'who's there', as if it's normal to be in there but it's not normal to come in unannounced," Brain said, poking his spaghetti. "It just doesn't seem right. I think it was someone else."

"It makez sense to me," Z said. "That dude waz pretty wack. He waz bein fishy from the start."

Jake looked over at me. "Gerald may be a sketchy dude but I don't think he's a spy. He goes to my school and we used to talk all the time before the teams."

Brain was studying the notebook. "I'm still trying to figure out what 'Twired Coyote Showcase' could possibly mean." He flipped through the pages.

"It seems like the camp is funding this thing," I said.

Time to clean up your tables!" Bill said to us, walking around the campers finishing their dinner.

We threw away our trash and walked toward our campsite "Sleepy Hollow." On the way over we kept talking.

"Iz think we should bez using our phones to figure thiz out," Z said walking over.

"I tried already but there is no cellular connection in the woods," Brain said.

"It's called Wi-Fi," Jake said under his breath. Brain rolled his eyes.

We sat around the campfire in the middle of the circle of shelters. "There's some random dots on this page but I don't know what they mean," Brain said looking at the notebook.

Z opened a bag of chips. "It lookz like musical notes broski."

Brain turned to look at him. "How?"

Z took a pencil out of my backpack.

"Hey!" I yelled.

"I'll give it backz, home hog, chillax." I groaned and nodded. He drew some lines on the dots which made notes in the treble clef. "A,D,E,B,A," he said, pointing with the pencil eraser.

"What do those letters mean? They're just dots," Jake said.

"But theyz be all on separate linez," he said. It was true. The dots were all on and between separate lines on the blue lined notebook paper. Making a musical clef.

"Is it a code for something?" Brain wondered out loud.

"Who cares about some letters?, Look at this." I grabbed the notebook from him and flipped to the page where it talked about Mikey being a cover for W.W. "Look here."

"Why would they call it a cover?" Brain said. "Wait! Mikey isn't real!"

Jake lowered his eyebrows. "Old news dude."

"No! The guy I saw in the woods, Julian! The one I thought was Mikey!" he told me.

I went wide eyed. "That wasn't Mikey!"

We both said together, "It was W.W.!"

BLUE RIBBONS

Everyone wants to wake up to, "We won, home hogz!" I wiped off Z's spit from my face.

"What?" I asked as I woke.

"We won the competition, broski!" Z said as he was smiling really hard. I got up and smacked my head on the wooden roof of my shelter, causing the sticks and wood pieces to fall down on top of me. Despite that, I was happier than ever.

"Woohoo!" I heard from across the field. Jake had two little confetti guns in his hands and was shooting ribbons out of them—blue ribbons.

"Where did ya get those?" I asked him, half chuckling.

"Bill brought some for if we won the competition!" he replied. I was surprised to see that Jake so happy. I didn't think he really cared about the competition. Or was much into any team events for that matter.

I was just happy that we actually won! All at once A rush of thoughts came to my head. How we got hurt so many times this past two weeks. Getting chased by a rolling tree, attacked by paint, almost drowning, rope burns, almost killing a fireman. It was just a lot! I was just glad that we did it.

I grabbed the plastic gun from Jake's hand and shot some ribbons and confetti into the air. Brain came out into the clearing as well wearing a purple Hawaiian shirt.

"We beat the Red Team?" he asked, just as surprised as we were.

"YES!" we all cheered. There were high-fives and fist bumps all around.

"Even with all the spies?" Brain said. I forgot about last night. We had figured out that the Twired Coyote Showcase was spying on the Blue Team.

"Did you figure out the anagram last night?" I asked him. Before he could answer, Z butted in front of me.

"Thanks for fixing upz mez shelter, Julian." I held out my hand and we did a secret handshake. I'd describe it for you because it was pretty complicated and really cool, but - it's a secret.

"No, I'm still trying to uncover what it means. If it even *is* an anagram. It could be something else," Brain said.

"Nice stuff, but who cares? We won! The spies failed, just celebrate," Jake said and shot out some more confetti. Bill came walking down the gravel trail with a huge golden trophy and a box.

"What's the box for, Bill?" I asked.

"You'll see," he said.

"Attention everyone on the Blue Team!" he announced. I'd like to take a moment to recap our incredible journey these past days. "On day five, we had a pretty strong battle but ended up losing that round.

Not to be deterred, on day six, we won that one pretty easily on the rope course.

We seemed unstoppable as we won the race up Mount Daisy! I could not have been any prouder or more excited. But the competition wasn't over.

I was a little disappointed with you guys at that race to the Magic Rock, though, you guys didn't even go to the finish line!" he said, chuckling.

It really seemed like anyone's competition and truthfully I thought this would be another Red

Team win - a streak I have been trying to break forever!

Your camp mate Julian knocked it out of the park with all of his clever work with the shelter-building contest, which sealed the deal for the Blue Team."

Everyone started clapping - not the pity claps you hear at school functions, but the genuine ones that give you goose bumps.

"Anyway, I have awards for some," he paused, "pretty awesome people." He then proceeded to pull out a trophy with every camper's name on it. As each trophy was passed out, Bill was sure to mention something good that they had done during their weeks at camp.

"Thankz," Z said with a wide grin when he got the last trophy.

I could see there were no more trophies left in the box. My heart sank. I'm not really a trophy collector sort of guy, but not getting one had me feeling pretty low despite being on the winning team. I felt like I was a big part of us winning. I briefly heard my parent's voices in my head. *Sometimes things don't work out the way we want them too and that's okay*.

"Sorry Julian, we ran out I guess," Bill said, trying to hide a smile.

Suddenly I knew what was happening. He pulled a trophy out from behind his back. "Julian Jimskipper, come get your reward!" Bill exclaimed. Everyone started cheering. Bill really had me going there. I grabbed the trophy from his hands and looked admiringly at it.

My Dad always said trophies were nothing more than a reminder that something in your past was good. I knew no matter what was going to happen to me in the future, I would always have reminders that my life was good and could be again.

WE FINALLY HAD NO MORE competition. That meant all the time that we had left here was to do anything we wanted.

We went fishing to catch some fish later on. We heard that the lake was actually stocked every Spring so there would be fish to catch. I ended up catching three rainbow trout—more than anyone else. I didn't tell anyone what I was using for bait, but apparently fish liked marshmallows almost as much as Z!

We finally did some archery as well, which I had wanted to do on the weaponry day all the way back at the beginning of camp. It probably won't surprise you, but I didn't get a bullseye.

"Julian you're supposed to *hit* the target!" Jake said, chuckling.

It felt like a more relaxed summer camp then. It was like the pressures of the competition and the pressures of life had just faded into the summer heat.

By lunch time we were telling the rest of Blue Team of our crazy adventures and how we survived so many truly zany things. Me, Jake, Z, and Brain talked about the Mystery of Mikey thing; which we had proved once and for all was untrue. We later told all the kids about the Mikey story and its bogus origins. And of course they didn't believe us and shrugged us off as conspiracy theorists.

"What shack? There's no shack out in the woods!" Some kids we were talking to started spouting animatedly.

We wove the elaborate tale about me getting lost in the woods and us discovering the notebook.

"Oh yeah? Where is the so called notebook then?" they asked.

I nervously scratched the back of my neck. "Well uh, it's in my backpack so I don't really want to dig it out right now." I told them, which I have to admit did not make my story any more believable.

"Yeah, *sure*," they said and walked off.

Amidst all the commotion and comings and goings of people, I looked up to the sky. The sun was starting its descent toward the horizon, not quite sunset yet, but it was getting there.

"Yo, home hog, they gotz some boatin' going on down at da beach! Ya wanna come?" Z asked me. I liked that people were thinking of me when they wanted to do something fun.

We went boating and this time I didn't almost drown, but I checked and then double checked to make sure the canoe didn't have any holes in it at all. "Thank god," I said when I didn't sink in the water. After some paddling around though I realized that it was kind of boring when you weren't racing. Nice, but boring.

I pushed my paddle through the water and brought the canoe over to the dock. I looked over my shoulder and saw that Z, Jake and Brain were still paddling around. I got in the water and swam near them. They were fairly close to shore and my feet were touching bottom. I jumped out of the water and startled Brain off of his canoe.

"Oh come on!" Brain exclaimed as he emerged from the water. He climbed back onto his canoe and tapped me on the shoulder with the paddle.

"Ow! Hey!" I moaned as we both started laughing.

Later on we even did a belly flop contest off the pier. It was all great. We were laughing and having fun and I felt like everything had really paid off.

At dinner we gave the final goodbye and enjoyed the last night of the camp. We all said grace and had our last meal together. I got a Caesar salad from the old lunch lady and I enjoyed that too. Everything tasted a bit better now. I enjoyed everything about that camp and when it was finally time to go back to our tents that we hadn't been in for days, I felt awesome. Like a hero returning from a quest.

When I was a little kid, I never liked superhero movies because I thought that they were so lame. I never liked how the heroes were always perfect. *A real hero isn't perfect. A real hero gets a couple trees thrown at them but they manage to get up and out of the way.*

At last it was finally time to leave. It was sunset and everyone was all saying their final goodbyes. The sun was peeking through the trees and the air felt cool but still warm. I finally felt like I was connected to a place. The crowds came together and broke apart. It looked like everyone had made friends here and bonded. I was sad to go, but it was also an experience to remember. Z, Jake, Brain and I stood together, saying goodbye.

"Bye home hogz... So long dudes... Goodbye my friends... Bye guys," we all said to each other. I pulled out my phone and took a picture to remember the four of us and have a memento for the road.

"Hey guys what are your numbers?" I asked. "Ya know, so we can all keep in touch." We all exchanged phone numbers so we could start a group chat. We called it the Fantastic Four. We all wanted to come back again next summer for sure, but now it was time to go. I obviously didn't want to leave after all I'd been through at camp.

I was a bit surprised when I saw my mom pull up alongside me and my friends in her new minivan. It was a nice silver color, and it had chrome plating on the doors and everything. She must have got it while I was gone. A pop song was playing on the radio.

"Woah, dude when did your mom get such a sweet ride!" Jake asked.

I shrugged and said, "It looks like things are finally going my way." Everyone laughed, remembering all the things that had definitely not gone my way.

Z smiled. "Don't getz too comfy."

I climbed in and patted the side of the car door

while the window was open. "See ya guys next year!"

"See ya, Julian!" Brain shouted back. The guy directing cars waved my mom through. Mom put the pedal to the metal and we went zooming out of there like a roller coaster. As we drove away I took one last look at the dusty old camp.

Bad things happen, but so do good things.

"Where is it?" Rick said, fumbling around his desk.

"I have no idea sir,." Joey told him, adjusting his camera.

"What are you missing?" Gerald asked him.

"The notebook and binder!" They're gone!"

Gerald thought for a minute. "Wait, I saw some kid take it! It was that dumb kid that broke my arm!" he said.

"Sprained your arm," Joey corrected, him while rolling his eyes.

"Julian!" Rick shouted. "He was the one that broke into the shack."

"Yeah, I told you I saw him running out of here the other day sir," Gerald remarked.

The "missing kid" opened the door and walked into the room. He typed the passcode next to the door.

"Is this alarm thing even necessary?" he asked. "You know, since Joey broke the door when he was in the firefighter suit getting the kid?"

"Shut it, Tim, we're in the middle of something," Joey whispered.

"If that kid finds out what we're doing we could be exposed!" Rick yelled.

Tim interjected, "The lookouts by Lumberjack Woods said they saw the notebook with him in his shelter, but after investigating, we've found nothing."

"You were supposed to guard the place, Gerald!" Joey accused.

"I was guarding the place! I have no idea how they got in without setting off the alarm!" He whined.

"It doesn't matter, we still lost and now Bill is gonna rub it in my face like he did all those years ago."

"Ugh, he's gonna tell it again," Gerald whispered to Joey.

"He beat me before, and I swore he would never do it again." Rick clenched his fist.

"You could have just gotten over that one loss instead of making a secret society," Gerald told him.

"I'm doing you a favor! You signed up to do the photography course here anyway!" Rick told him, standing up. "And plus, I have a plan to get the notebook back."

"And what would that be, sir?" Tim asked.

Rick smiled. "Send a letter to Julian Jimskipper. Ask him if he would like to join us this October for the Camp Golden Hills fall festival."

ACKNOWLEDGMENTS

I would like to thank my Teacher, Mrs. Nosel, and the rest of the period one class. This book originally started as a school assignment which was to write a novel in one month. I created the basic shape of this story but of course shorter and not quite as developed. Without her I would never have pursued my love of writing.

I would also like to thank my editor Kelsy Thompson for believing that a good book could become a great book. She helped me throughout each stage of the book development and challenged me to put more detail into it. Doing this, I felt like the characters in the book were people I've known for a long time. The character's personalities and story lines could not have been as thought out as they were if not for Kelsy.

A huge part of the inspiration to this book was from my Boy Scout Troop 175 in MA. Going to camping and hiking trips year-round, we had a lot of crazy things happen. Amplifying and exaggerating them created an amazing story. All the people in the troop helped make this story come to life. Thank you, guys, so much for helping me with this story, even though you didn't know it!

I also want to thank my brother Michael and sister Connie. They test read the book and were the first people other than my parents to read the school assigned book. Without their constant thirst to have the final version of my novel I might have never finished the book.

Julian in the book made a group chat called Fantastic 4. One of the greatest friend groups I ever had was the real Fantastic 5. They made me laugh all the time, and a lot of the lunch parts in the story were exaggerated memories of my friend group. Thank you so much.

Best for last, I also couldn't have done this story without my Mom and Dad who helped me so much throughout the book, and even gave me the idea to make it a real novel! Every day my Dad was right next to me reminding me of ideas and events that could be sprinkled into the book to make it interesting. My Mom gave me ideas and helped me make decisions in the book. Without you guys the book never could have happened and it might have just stayed a school assignment. You guys are the reason this book was made, so thank you so much!

ABOUT THE AUTHOR

Daniel Currier is a 13-year-old student at Mountview Middle School. He is a Boy Scout, who goes camping & hiking a lot. He plays the piano and also plays the trumpet in his school band.

With a strong talent for creating a world full of lovable characters, it's not a surprise that eventually he would create the book that you have now. This is Daniel's first book.

www.daniel-currier.com

Also available as an ebook.
Photo by Todd Mandella. 2019.